A
Regency
Romp

Three novellas
plus
Three short stories

A Regency Romp

LEIGH MICHAELS

PBL Limited
Ottumwa, Iowa

A Regency Romp
copyright 2016, 2024 by Leigh Michaels

Characters in this book have no existence outside the imagination of the author. This is a work of fiction.

An Unlucky Match copyright 2015
Her Wedding Wager copyright 2015
An Affair for the Season copyright 2013
Wedding Daze copyright 2011
The Tattooed Lady copyright 2010
Blind Date copyright 2012

Contents

An Unlucky Match (short novella)   ~ 7

Her Wedding Wager (novella)   ~ 42

An Affair for the Season (novella) ~ 114

Wedding Daze (short story)   ~ 171

The Tattooed Lady (short story)   ~ 187

Blind Date (short-short story)   ~ 198

An Unlucky Match

Here we go again, Audra Lambton told herself as she turned from watching the dancers and found herself suddenly face to face – well, nose to beak, really – with London's most notorious gossip.

"Lady Audra," the woman repeated. "I asked if you are dreaming of days gone by."

Audra asked herself why she hadn't just walked on, pretending not to hear. Possibly because it was so rare for Lady Stone's gravelly tones to be mixed with anything which resembled compassion. The old woman's opinions were generally every bit as sharp as her nose, which seemed to precede her into any room.

Audra sighed inwardly, while pasting a smile onto her face. "I beg your pardon, Lady Stone. Were you speaking to me?"

"Are you regretting your lost love? I couldn't help but notice that you were watching Lord Kinley waltzing with that milksop of an heiress."

"I wasn't…" The protest was automatic – and foolish, Audra realized, for she *had* been watching Lord Kinley as he circled the dance floor. And pure bad luck it was that the very first festivity she attended on her return to London was also the first time Audra had been in the same room with Lucas Kinley since their betrothal had ended abruptly last spring.

But in truth, whether they bumped into each other on the dance floor or stayed at opposite sides of the room all evening would make little difference. The *ton* gossips would have a grand time speculating, and Lady Stone seemed to want a head start.

"Of course, love – or the loss of it – doesn't seem to be hurting *him*," Lady Stone added.

"There was never any question of love between us," Audra said before she could stop herself.

Lady Stone's gaze sharpened. "No one would deny that your betrothal was a very *sensible* arrangement, at least on Lord Kinley's side. Such a pity about his father and that unfortunate gambling problem. At least the man had the good taste to die before the family was *quite* washed up, though one does wonder..."

"Whether the situation was even worse than the *ton* knew, to make Lord Kinley take the risk of betrothing himself to me?" Audra willed her tone to remain steady. "A simply enormous dowry will make a gentleman overlook all kinds of warning signs."

"Yes, it will – at least for a while." Lady Stone clucked her tongue. "Come now; don't look at me as though I'm spitting toads, for I only said what you yourself are obviously thinking. But it's foolish to believe your ill luck has made you some sort of antidote, Audra. As soon as word spreads that you have returned to town–"

"Since I am in London only because my brother's ward requires a chaperone, the gentlemen need not bother to call on me." Audra curtseyed. "Your pardon, Lady Stone, but I must catch up with my charge and make certain she is not embarrassing the duke."

"Is she likely to?" Lady Stone's beady gaze grew brighter.

Audra cursed her wayward tongue. Now everyone who mattered would be even more attentive to her charge's conduct.

As Audra turned away, she heard Lady Stone murmur once more, "One does wonder..."

What was the old woman about to say? *One does wonder why Lady Audra has agreed to take part in another Season at all, even from the fringes of the* ton? *One does wonder why the Duke of Melksham trusts the well-being of his ward to his sister, when she couldn't bring her own betrothal – any one of them – to a successful conclusion?*

"I don't care," Audra muttered. Even though the Season seemed to stretch out before her to infinity, it would not last forever. And by the end of her three months in London, with her brother's ward successfully established, Audra herself would be set for life.

Melksham had promised.

She felt the ripples in her wake as she crossed the ballroom and thought she could almost hear the whispers.

"That's Lady Audra Lambton over there. She's been betrothed three times, and they all died.*"*

"Not all. *The first two died, yes. One of consumption, I believe, and the other of pneumonia. But the third –"*

" – suffered from pleurisy, and my mama says he had one foot actually in the grave and the other scrabbling for purchase on the edge when he came to his senses."

"Who can blame him for crying off? Though I understand he was so ill he could barely croak the words which released him!"

And then came the play on her name which always set Audra's teeth on edge, for it was delivered as a sort of Greek chorus, dripping with hypocritical sympathy and horrified glee: *"That Poor Lamb!"*

Audra held her head higher. Across the room her charge – the very lively Miss Dorinda Grey – was holding court, surrounded by young men. *At least I needn't fret that Dorinda will be a wallflower.*

A gentleman in severe black evening garb beckoned imperiously. Audra considered pretending not to see him, but she could hardly ignore her brother, so she strolled over to where he stood in the shadow of a pillar.

The Duke of Melksham barely spared her a glance, for he was staring through his quizzing glass at his ward and her court. "Dorinda seems to have set out to collect fribbles, fops, and penniless younger sons. What do you plan to do about that, Audra?"

"I'm not going to drag her away, for that would only make the attraction stronger on both sides."

"I want her well-settled – and soon."

"Yes, Mellie, you've made yourself quite plain. Please remember I want a happy outcome for Dorinda as much as you do."

Melksham's gaze drifted across the ballroom. "What about you, Audra? See anyone out there who appeals?"

Audra stared at him. Had he conveniently forgotten their agreement? Or had he been listening at all while she explained her terms? She should have suspected that Melksham had been just a shade too amenable when he surrendered.

Or had this been his plan all along – agree to anything she asked, but once Audra was back in London, try again to marry her off? How foolish to think her only challenge this Season would be dealing with the empty-headed Dorinda!

"Despite our agreement? Oh, why not, Mellie?" Audra let sarcasm creep into her voice. "But since I don't care to choose, you must let me know if there is someone in particular – someone who has offended you, perhaps? – that you'd *like* me to kill next."

A low, rich laugh behind her sent shivers up Audra's spine. What was she thinking, to snap at her brother in public?

She had recognized the laugh, of course – though that hardly made the situation better. She slowly turned to confront Lucas Kinley. Thank heaven he no longer had the milksop heiress in tow.

Her former betrothed looked as delicious as ever. He was taller than Melksham and not at all inclined to the paunch which gave the duke's tailor nightmares. Lucas was far more exotic, too – with deep brown eyes and hair so dark it seemed to absorb, rather than reflect, candlelight from the nearby sconces. Audra had always thought there must be a Spaniard – or perhaps a pirate! – somewhere in his family tree.

She realized she was staring and said coolly, "You're looking …" *Handsome? Appealing? Tempting?* – Not to her, of course, but she could understand this year's crop of damsels going quite mad for his dark good looks. "… well."

He bowed. "I am in excellent health, my lady."

No thanks to you, Audra. He might as well have said it.

"I am told you do not dance this evening, Lady Audra, but perhaps you will make an exception for me."

"And cause a good deal of talk amongst the gossips? I think not."

"You'll cause even more talk if you refuse," Lucas pointed out. "Let us be seen together, enjoying a simple dance, and everyone will realize there's nothing to chatter about."

"Clearly you don't know the gossips. I attended this event only to chaperone my brother's ward."

"It appears Lady Stone has Miss Grey in hand," Lucas said.

Audra peered past him. That combination spelled disaster if the naïve Dorinda, flattered by the attention of one of the *ton*'s lions, was to babble. *Oh, dear.*

"That's a good point, Audra," Melksham put in. "Lady Stone will keep a careful eye on Dorinda – and since you've left her alone for the last half hour, the length of a waltz can do no further harm. Go and dance with Lucas."

That showed how much Melksham knew about it – but Dorinda's damage was probably already done. Audra's waltz with Lord Kinley, on the other hand…

Of course he had chosen a waltz. Not for the romantic appeal, Audra suspected, but because in just a few minutes spent sweeping around the ballroom together – with no interruptions, no changing partners – they would draw the gaze of every person in attendance. At least the whole thing would be over in a flash – unlike a country dance which might go on for half an hour.

They made the first circle of the floor in silence before he said, "You might consider a smile, Lady Audra."

"Why? So the gossips can speculate about whether I'm trying to ensnare you once more?"

"*Are* you trying to ensnare me?"

"Of course not!"

"Then smile and confuse them."

She shot him the most insincere grimace she could muster. "You realize everyone in this room thinks you're the one who broke off our betrothal, but that you insisted it was my idea simply to preserve my good name?"

But what else could people possibly think, given the circumstances? Lucas *was* too much the gentleman to allow a lady to be known as a jilt. Of course, he was also sensitive to his own reputation, and a gentleman could never back out of a marriage arrangement. Idly, she wondered how much longer he'd have let the betrothal go on, had she not called a halt in the nick of time to save his life.

Revolving around the floor meant Audra could see every one of the gossips watching her. "I wish you had left me in obscurity to chaperone."

"*You*, Audra? If you wanted to be obscure, why are you here rather than in Derbyshire?"

"Because our aunt, who was to sponsor Dorinda, is suffering from rheumatism, so at the last minute Melksham asked me to step in."

"I don't recall rheumatism giving your aunt pause when she was chaperoning *you*." He let another circle of the floor go by. "You mentioned an agreement. I'm curious – what did you ask of Melksham in return for your services?"

Freedom, Audra almost said, before she caught herself. "Belgian lace. Norwich shawls. An absolutely spanking new fur. The usual things."

He looked doubtful, but the waltz ended before he could challenge her. Just in time, too. Dorinda wasn't the only one who would benefit from learning to mind her tongue.

Audra curtseyed and deliberately pitched her voice to be overheard. "So pleasant to see you again, my lord. I hope you will have an enjoyable Season." With a final – and this time genuine – smile, she headed toward the corner of the ballroom where she'd last seen Dorinda.

And that, Audra thought, was that. The word would spread that Lord Kinley and *That Poor Lamb* Audra Lambton had shared a single dance, a few minutes of pleasant conversation, and a whole wagonload of good will. With nothing to chatter about, the gossips would move on, and so could Audra. Perhaps the waltz had been a good idea after all.

She turned her thoughts to Dorinda and the challenge of finding the young woman a match high enough to satisfy the Duke of Melksham. Considering that Dorinda was nearly as lacking in dowry as she was in common sense, finding her a title and a fortune would be easier said than done.

As Audra strolled through the crowd, however, smiling until her jaw ached, she began to get the glimmer of an idea that might solve Dorinda's problem – and her own, as well.

*****

The young gentlemen who called on Dorinda Grey the next day at the Duke of Melksham's house on Grosvenor Square were exactly the sort Audra had expected – and feared. Melksham was correct to dismiss them as fribbles, fops, and penniless younger sons. The only title in the bunch was a mere baron who possessed almost no property. Dorinda herself seemed most starry-eyed over the red coats of a couple of soldiers – neither of them above the rank of captain. Then there was the contingent of young men who made a habit of attending the Beauty of the Season, whoever she might be. Audra had enjoyed their attentions in her own first Season, three years ago, but she'd known better than to take any of them seriously. She wasn't certain Dorinda would be as perceptive.

Three years ago. That was the Season Audra had fallen head over heels in love with Viscount Wornell, the second of her unfortunate betrotheds – the one who had overturned his curricle in a snowstorm during a particularly ill-advised race from London to Bath, lain in a drift for an hour or more with a couple of broken ribs, and ultimately died of pneumonia.

Audra shivered as if she'd found herself in the midst of that swirling wetness.

Enough, she reminded. Viscount Wornell was part of her past. She couldn't go back and fix things, but she would not repeat her mistakes.

While she watched over Dorinda's callers, Audra entertained herself by working out her plan. It was simple enough that she'd covered every detail by the time the callers departed. She patted back a yawn – this chaperoning business was tedious in the extreme – and gave permission for Dorinda to walk in the park with a group of young women.

When the butler announced Lord Kinley, Audra wondered for an instant whether she had conjured him up out of her own desires, for she had been debating how to get his ear for a private talk. Her insides fluttered at the first glimpse of his dark good looks.

Before she could ask what had brought him to Grosvenor Square, he was making his bow. "You seem startled to see me, Lady Audra."

"I expected you to be calling on Miss Gardiner."

His eyes lit. "How flattering that you noticed with whom I danced last evening."

Well, that reaction wasn't what I expected. "I was contemplating the fact that your partner is best known for the plumpness of her dowry."

"You are unkind to point out that I am still as much in need of funds as I was last year." But Lucas didn't sound injured, only matter-of-fact.

"It *would* be rude of me to bring up your financial circumstances, if I didn't have a plan in mind."

"What sort of plan? I understand *your* dowry is still available."

Audra snapped, "I am no more interested in renewing our betrothal than you are."

"I'm glad to have that matter cleared up. But I meant only that last night I overheard Melksham talking to Whitman about your dowry. I must warn you, Whitman didn't seem keen on the notion."

"That cad!" She noted the way Lucas's eyebrow quirked. "Not Whitman, of course. One can hardly blame him for being lukewarm, considering my record. But I thought I'd made myself clear to Mellie last night – *again*."

"Ah, yes. I suspect your agreement has very little to do with Belgian lace and… was it Norwich shawls? What is this plan you're hatching?"

Audra took a deep breath and leaned forward. "Can I trust you?"

"With your life, my dear," he drawled.

"Very funny." She paused, toying with her ratafia glass. "You don't want to marry Miss Gardiner."

"You sound as though you have a right to an opinion."

Audra felt color rising in her cheeks. "That's not what I mean. I have an alternate suggestion. I think you should marry Dorinda."

"Why would I want to?" Lucas said baldly.

"For one thing, she has a chin – unlike Miss Gardiner."

"But Miss Grey has no dowry to speak of. Deep though Melksham's pockets are, he's not likely to sweeten the portion of a mere ward."

"That's where I come in. You're correct that my agreement with my brother does *not* involve my wardrobe. Melksham has promised me that if... *when* he announces Dorinda's betrothal to a titled gentleman of whom he approves, he will hand over to me the control of my entire dowry."

Lucas gave a low whistle.

"As you have reason to know, that's a great deal more money than I would actually need – far more than Miss Gardiner can claim. I am prepared to make up the shortfall in Dorinda's dowry with my own funds."

"Why would you agree to give away your money just because Melksham is trying to marry you off? My dear girl, why not just wait him out? You can say *No* more forcefully than any other lady I've ever known."

"Because of Dorinda," she admitted. "I realize now that making a match for her is likely to be...difficult."

Something glinted in Lucas's eyes. Audra hoped it was humor, but she suspected it was more like annoyance.

"And you think a handsome settlement means I wouldn't mind finding myself leg-shackled to her? The lack of a chin is one thing, Audra, but the lack of a brain—"

"Dorinda is not actually dim. She's just very young and a bit bubble-headed and likely to fall in love with all the wrong men, while the right sort are apt to dismiss her without a second thought. But if a solid, sensible, and steady gentleman were to offer for her..."

"A solid, sensible, and steady gentleman like me?"

Audra said reasonably, "Since Melksham found you to be a suitable match for the sister of a duke, I have no doubt he'd turn handsprings in glee if you offered for his ward."

"Let's keep count, shall we? That would make you and Melksham happy, while Dorinda and I would be anything but. Something seems awry with this bargain."

Audra smiled at him. "How do you know you wouldn't be the happiest couple in England? You're doing exactly as I expected, dismissing Dorinda without knowing anything about her – when in fact, I promise you will find her quite engaging when you get to know her."

Lucas stared at her as though she'd sprouted horns.

Before he could regain the power of speech, Audra pressed her advantage. "You'll have your chance tonight, when you come to dinner. We'll be attending the Renfrews' ball afterwards. I presume you are going as well?"

*****

Audra was very careful not to arouse Dorinda's hopes when she mentioned that Lord Kinley would be their guest at dinner, describing him as a friend of Melksham's and not as a potential suitor. Her caution was rewarded, because the girl was at her most delightful all through the evening. Delightful, at least, by Dorinda standards. She giggled now and then, and – truth be told – her eyes glazed over during the sweet course when Lucas told her about the efficient farming methods he planned to implement on his Sussex estate when he returned there after the Season.

But dinner was a success, and Audra congratulated herself at the Renfrews' ball when Lucas signed his name on Dorinda's dance card before turning to Audra herself. "And don't tell me you aren't dancing," he said, "because we shall need a way to conspire without drawing attention to ourselves."

She laughed and said she'd be looking forward to it, and watched him go off to partner Dorinda in the first country dance.

"You and Lord Kinley seem to be on the best of terms," Lady Stone observed shrewdly over the rim of her punch cup. "I see he has not asked Miss Gardiner for her dance card this evening."

"Really?" Audra said calmly. "Perhaps he agrees with you that she's a bit of a milksop."

When the time came for Lucas to present himself for their waltz, Audra took his arm and said, "I think it would be better if we just walk around the room."

He guided her into the crowd of dancers instead. "When we're moving so quickly around the floor, no one can overhear."

Audra had to admit he had a point – one never knew, for instance, where Lady Stone might pop up, and the woman seemed to have the ears of a bat. Besides, Lucas did dance beautifully – Audra had always thought so, and now that they were once more at ease with each other, she had the sense she was floating around the room in his arms. She was tall for a woman, but with Lucas she felt tiny and fragile – and her golden-brown hair and pale green dress formed a striking contrast to his dark good looks. "What do you think of Dorinda now?"

"Sharing a country dance hardly makes for a fair appraisal of her qualities."

"True enough, but you have asked for a second dance, have you not? I will give permission for her to sit with you rather than dancing."

"If I were to try to peel her away from her troop of admirers for a *tete-a-tete*, every matron in the *ton* would have us betrothed before the evening was out."

What would be so wrong with that? But Audra knew better than to say it. "What do you suggest? If you require further acquaintance before making your decision..."

"Silly of me, perhaps, to want to exchange more than a few words with a prospective bride before making a formal offer, but there it is. I propose you take the young lady shopping tomorrow."

"Shopping?" Audra said doubtfully.

"I shall encounter you along Bond Street, and you may commandeer me to carry your boxes and bundles."

"And by the time we've shopped the length of the street, you'll know all you need to about Dorinda. What a perfectly capital idea!" She smiled up at him and felt the breath catch in her throat at how very handsome he was.

*****

After being stuck in Derbyshire for the greater part of a year, Audra should have thought of a visit to Bond Street herself. Dorinda, of course, was eager for a shopping trip, though her pin money seemed to have been spent long since. That was just as well, for the girl's tastes were unreliable.

"The shape of that bonnet is all wrong for you," Audra pointed out when Dorinda stopped to admire the display in a milliner's window, just as Lucas tipped his hat to them. "And the orange ribbons would clash with your hair. Good morning, my lord."

Dorinda gave a girlish pout. "Lord Kinley, is it not unkind of my chaperone to call attention to the unfortunate color of my hair?"

"You should give thanks to have a lady of such notable taste shaping your opinions, child."

Audra didn't know whether to be pleased that he had complimented her taste or annoyed because he was acting toward Dorinda like an elderly uncle.

"And I find the color of your hair to be unexceptional, Miss Grey," he went on, "much closer to blonde than the red which Lady Audra seemed to indicate." Dorinda preened, but Lucas had already turned to Audra. "May I offer assistance with your bundles?"

She handed over her purchases and said slyly, "If we had realized we would find quite so many treasures this morning, we'd have brought a footman. But I expect you'll do quite nicely as a substitute, my lord."

Dorinda moved on to the next shop, where she admired a truly garish necklace.

Lucas leaned closer. "You tempt me to remember some pressing engagement."

Audra let a tremor creep into her voice. "I quake at the threat."

He laughed, rearranged the packages so he could offer his arm, and patiently walked them up and down the length of the street. Eventually, he handed Dorinda into a hackney and piled the packages around her, then offered his hand to Audra to help her climb in.

She paused and said softly, "What do you think now?"

"I believe further investigation is required."

"We're promised at a musicale this evening, if you'd care to join us." He winced, and Audra laughed. "Very well – I won't require you to attend. Dinner instead?"

Lucas shook his head. "Two nights in a row? What would the gossips say? Let's ride tomorrow. At least I assume Miss Grey does not fear horses?"

"Of course she doesn't. Ten o'clock along Rotten Row?"

He bowed assent and helped her into the hackney. As Audra settled herself amongst the bundles, Dorinda slid back from her perch on the edge of the seat. Had the child been peering out, trying to catch a last glimpse of her new suitor?

"Do you like him, Lady Audra?"

"Certainly, dear." Audra kept her tone careless.

Dorinda beamed. "Good. Then we shall see him again soon." She leaned her forehead against the window and began to hum.

The sound scratched on Audra's nerves. Really, why did the child not realize how very annoying a tuneless little hum could be? She settled back to do a little dreaming of her own.

With full control of her fortune, Audra could live anywhere she liked. Not in Derbyshire, of course. She loved Lambton Castle, but settling too close to her brother's country seat would tempt Melksham to continue poking his nose into her life. If she was not going home, however, she could choose a more temperate climate and a town large enough to keep her busy and entertained.

Brighton, perhaps. It was lively, with the Prince Regent and his cronies coming and going – though was it perhaps *too* lively for a gentlewoman living alone?

Dorinda giggled and waved at someone on the street. Audra looked out the window to see Lucas strolling along the pavement, no doubt on his way to his club. What was the child thinking to behave like a hoyden? Audra hadn't expected to have to rein in the girl's daydreams – not yet, at any rate. It simply wouldn't do, if Dorinda began to act as if Lucas already belonged to her!

*****

Dorinda did well enough while riding in the park, but crowded conditions meant that the three of them couldn't ride abreast. When one of her soldiers came up to them, Dorinda spurred ahead, leaving Lucas and Audra to follow. "She does have a good command of her mount," Audra observed.

"Acceptable, but she'd benefit from studying your example."

Audra couldn't help but be pleased at the compliment. Perhaps she was vain, she admitted, but she had always shown to advantage on horseback and it was nice to know someone noticed. Of course she shouldn't encourage him to unfavorably compare Dorinda with anyone. "I believe I owe you my thanks, by the way. Melksham told me he will make no further efforts to arrange my future."

"That's considerate of him." Lucas frowned. "Why do you think I had any part in that?"

"When I asked him why he had changed his mind, he said – somewhat clumsily, it is true – that you pointed out how embarrassing it would be for me if he was observed to be shopping me around to numerous gentlemen."

"I said nothing of the kind. I suggested you're capable of making your own decisions, as long as he leaves off interfering."

She smiled. "I didn't think it likely you'd phrased it in quite the way Mellie did. Nevertheless, it seems to have had the desired effect."

He rode on in silence. "You really have no desire to marry, ever?"

"Of course I don't. Perhaps that's why my betrothals have all been ill-fated – because the gentlemen realized how reluctant I was, even though I myself was not aware of it. So they took any means of escaping me."

He said quietly, "This seems a poor subject for a jest."

She bit her lip hard, and tears stung her eyes for a moment. Did he really think she was flippant about the men who had died, or the fact that he himself had almost succumbed? "I'm sorry. I never meant you ill, Lucas, and I swear if I'd realized what a terrible nemesis I was, I'd never have agreed to our betrothal. But I thought… Well, I assumed it was only men I fell in love with who were in danger from the Poor Lamb's Curse."

"You're referring to Wornell. The story of that fiery courtship is a legend in the *ton*. But what about Alexander Shelburne? Did you love him as well?"

"In a schoolgirl-crush sort of way. I was only sixteen when he died, but I had always known that our fathers intended us to marry, and he was romantic in a Byronesque style. You know what I mean – pale and languid and so very poetic."

"I imagine that was the consumption showing itself, Audra, and not his true nature. Perhaps I should be thankful you didn't care as much for me."

He sounded perfectly good-humored about it. *There was never any question of love between us,* she had told Lady Stone. But that was no excuse for not realizing the danger she was putting him in, until it was almost too late.

"I was fond of you, Lucas. I still am." Her voice seemed to catch in her throat, and she added hastily, "Who would have thought we would become such good friends? It's just as well you're not nourishing a *tendre* for me. How very uncomfortable it would be to marry…" She caught his eye and swallowed the name she'd been about to say. "…one woman while doting on another. We must pick up our pace, however, before Dorinda's escort carelessly leads her out into the street."

Audra touched her horse's flank with her heel and pushed ahead of him. For the rest of the ride, she remained close to Dorinda's side, and she kept the conversation light and careless and far away from betrothals – either past or potential.

*****

They saw Lucas nearly every day after that – sometimes in the park, sometimes at a soiree or a ball. On a couple of evenings he came to dinner, appearing at the last minute when Melksham brought him home from some masculine entertainment.

On every occasion, Audra watched Dorinda carefully to gauge her reaction, and she had to admit she was pleased. The girl seemed to light up when Lucas was near, and he could win her to laughter more quickly than anyone else could.

A week or so later, as he and Audra were sitting out a country dance on the Allinghams' terrace, Lucas admitted he found Dorinda quite amusing. "A nice enough child, I admit – and her chatter is always enlightening."

"Didn't I promise you'd find her engaging? I suppose you'll be looking for an opportunity to discuss her future with Melksham." Audra kept her voice light, but inside she was confused. This was exactly what she'd wanted – wasn't it?

"Let the girl have her Season."

"That's… thoughtful of you." Audra let her fingertips trail across the chilly stone balustrade. "It's true that a betrothal changes things, and if this is to be her only Season–"

"Then it would be a shame to cut her enjoyment short."

"Besides, I have given my promise to make things come right for you, so there's no need to rush." She smiled up at him, relieved. "At least I can atone for the mess I made of your life last year, by making your dreams come true."

Lucas took her hand and pulled her up from the stone balustrade to stand beside him, just as another couple came through the long windows onto the terrace.

After the cold stone, Lucas's fingers seemed to burn hers even through her glove, and Audra was so close she could feel his breath stirring the hair at her temple. If she tipped her head back, his lips would brush against her face...

She said unsteadily, "We should go inside."

Lucas glanced down the terrace toward the other couple and then offered his arm.

How very foolish to let herself be distracted like that, when her goal was so nearly attained!

*****

The next day, Lucas presented himself as the ladies were receiving callers. Dorinda's following had grown with each passing week, and the throng of young men surrounding her was so noisy that Lucas quickly came to sit with Audra instead.

She looked up from her sketch of a needlepoint design for a chair cover. "I could have warned that flirting with Dorinda is impossible under these circumstances." She rubbed out an errant line.

"Then it is as well I didn't plan on doing anything of the sort today."

Audra forgot her sketch. "You must have had a purpose, to brave the tedious routine of morning calls."

"I am planning a small dinner party. Nothing so grand as the entertainment you have offered me, certainly, for I have only an ordinary cook whose skills are nothing like those of Melksham's chef. Also, the surroundings at Kinley House are, I fear, somewhat worn and tired. But if you would bear with me – along with Miss Grey and the duke, of course – I would be honored."

Audra was startled. But of course he would want Dorinda to see his home, where she would live whenever they came to London. "We are pleased to accept, and you must not apologize. I find the company at a party to be far more important than the menu or the decoration." She barely heard what she was saying.

Had there been something different about the way Lucas had said her brother's name this time? Despite what he'd told her about allowing Dorinda to have an entire Season before settling down to a betrothal, he must mean he was ready to declare himself – privately at least. Speaking to Melksham didn't mean he would immediately make his declaration to his chosen bride, of course – but once the details were arranged, he could ask Dorinda officially when the time was right.

That must be why Audra's midsection had that sudden all-gone feeling. Despite her determination, she'd hardly believed she could actually bring it off – and even now, she would not let herself count on success. Something could still happen to throw all her plans awry.

*****

Audra's own betrothal to Lucas Kinley had been so brief there had never been time for a visit to Kinley House, so she had to admit curiosity as the duke's town carriage drew up in Berkeley Square and Lucas's footman admitted them.

Dorinda looked around the entrance hall with childish anticipation followed by an equally obvious disappointment. "I thought it would be grander," she whispered. "It all looks a bit tired somehow."

"It's out of date, yes. But the rooms are beautifully proportioned, and things like hangings and carpets and chair covers are easy to replace."

"Perhaps Lord Kinley will ask for your help, Lady Audra," Dorinda observed.

A curl of anticipation ran through Audra. How she would love to clear out the age-faded fabrics, lighten the dark walls, add some brightness to the rooms… but that honor would fall to Lord Kinley's wife. To Dorinda.

Audra remembered the bonnet Dorinda had admired on their Bond Street expedition, the one with the ghastly orange ribbons, and shivered at the picture which formed in her mind of these grand old rooms done up in Dorinda's slapdash sense of fashion.

"Are you chilly, Lady Audra?" Lucas himself had come to greet them at the top of the stairs, to show them into the drawing room.

"Not at all." *Only fearing for the welfare of your house,* she wanted to say. She paused on the threshold. "Are we your only guests?" If only the four of them were present, then when the ladies retired after dinner, he and Melksham could settle the entire thing over the port without even needing to cross the hall to Lucas's library.

"And limit you to my poor company for an entire evening? Hardly. My other guests will be along shortly, I believe."

Even as he spoke, Audra heard a commotion downstairs, and two young men in uniform – the two most persistent of Dorinda's soldiers – soon joined them.

She sent a chiding look in Lucas's direction. He seemed not to see her as he went about making the young men – and Dorinda, of course – at home.

Before long, however, Audra saw the sense behind his invitation. It was all a matter of contrast; the two soldiers seemed young and pitifully callow next to the worldly and well-established Lord Kinley. His house might be in need of redecoration, but it was solid and huge and located on one of London's best squares. The lodgings of a mere soldier – even an officer – could not compare.

It was possible, however, Audra thought, that Lucas was giving Dorinda too much credit for subtlety, if he expected her to notice the finely-drawn comparison he had presented.

The last guest to arrive was Lady Stone, who had brought her companion.

"It wasn't exactly my idea," Lucas murmured into Audra's ear as he offered his arm to escort her in to dinner. "Lady Stone volunteered to act as my hostess."

Lady Stone, walking just ahead of them on the Duke of Melksham's arm, gave her bray of a laugh. "Someone needs to keep you in line, Lord Kinley. Audra dear, you must bring Miss Grey around the square to visit me tomorrow."

"I must? I mean – certainly, Lady Stone. What is the occasion?"

"I have a visitor from France who has offered to teach a few of my little friends the very latest in dances. Miss Grey would be devastated to be left behind."

Dorinda gave a crow of delight, and throughout dinner, it seemed, she could talk of nothing else. Audra tried to catch her charge's eye to signal a warning – but perhaps she, too, had given Dorinda too much credit for picking up nuances, because the chatter continued. Audra smothered a sigh and turned back to Lucas.

"She's young," Audra said, and wondered if she would have done better to press for an early betrothal rather than agreeing that Dorinda deserved to have a full Season before she was expected to settle down.

"Ennui has become fashionable among the younger set," Lucas said, "but I find your charge delightful and I applaud you for not breaking her spirit."

The note of indulgent approval in his voice ought to relieve Audra's mind. Clearly Lucas approved of Dorinda and the way his courtship was shaping up. What was wrong with Audra, that she didn't feel the same?

*****

After their return to Melksham House, Audra sent Dorinda up to bed and braved her brother in his library, waiting patiently until the duke stopped stirring papers on his desk and looked up at her.

"Well?" she said. "Did you and Lucas discuss ... arrangements?"

He harrumphed.

"Mellie," she warned, "don't you dare say it isn't my business."

"Oh, very well, then. Yes, we talked. But I'm not going to tell you any more than that. I swore I wouldn't breathe a word, for Lucas intends to handle things in his own time."

"But it's definitely settled?"

"Oh, yes." But the duke looked uneasy, and the way he dipped his pen in the inkwell made it clear he would say no more, so Audra gave it up and went to her room.

She was happy to have it all arranged. Her sense of unease no doubt arose from concern over her brother's odd reaction. She wondered if, in order to convince the duke his offer was serious, Lucas had had to admit the outlines of their private agreement to supplement Dorinda's dowry. If so, then Audra supposed she owed Lucas her thanks for extracting a promise from Melksham not to rake her over the coals – as he must have been sorely tempted to do – for making such a bargain.

Once again, it seemed, Lucas had her best interests at heart. As well as his own, of course.

*****

Lady Stone's informal dancing school involved a couple of dozen young people – not enough to crowd her ballroom, but a respectable gathering for such an impromptu occasion – along with a three-piece orchestra and a couple of tables groaning under the weight of tiny cakes and tempting treats. The food alone explained why the young men actually outnumbered the girls, and Audra conceded that Lady Stone was a wily old bird to manage that feat.

Audra herself was soon pressed into service as partner to one of the young captains who had been hovering around Dorinda. He and his companion had also attended Lucas's dinner party the previous night, when Dorinda had begged Lady Stone to invite them to the dancing party.

Audra had pulled her charge aside for a scold regarding her lack of manners, but Lady Stone said indulgently, "The more the merrier, my dear. By all means, bring along anyone you care to invite." And so here they were.

Audra had to admit the young soldier was earnest and shyly respectful, touching her as though she was breakable and as old as Lady Stone. Except for her feet; she had to hope for the young man's sake that he was more nimble in dodging enemy blows than he was on the dance floor. And she was very glad she hadn't worn her brand-new pair of dancing slippers to the party, for by the time the music stopped, Audra's shoes were quite scuffed from contact with the Captain's boots, and she was relieved to move on to another partner.

Finally, happily exhausted, the youngsters took their departure in small groups, and Dorinda sank gracefully onto a bench at the edge of the ballroom to change her slippers for walking boots for their trek across the square.

"I shall always remember this party, Lady Stone," Dorinda said.

Lady Stone sipped a glass of port – Audra had politely refused to join her – and said, "What shall you recall most clearly, Miss Grey?"

Dorinda blushed and looked down and said finally, "It's the first time I've been really certain that I care for James – Captain Andrews – above all the others."

Audra's jaw dropped. "But a match of that sort is just not possible, Dorinda. What about Lord Kinley?"

"What about him?"

Was the girl really as dim as she sounded? "It's all understood, my dear. You shall marry him."

Dorinda's eyes rounded. "Lord Kinley? But he's so *old*!"

"Nonsense. A few years difference between husband and wife is to be desired. A mature gentleman is more stable, more certain of what he wants."

Dorinda shook her head. "But he's not what *I* want!"

Audra couldn't believe her ears.

"Are you quite certain, Audra dear," Lady Stone asked gently, "that you wouldn't like that glass of port after all?"

Audra had been so caught up in Dorinda's foolishness that momentarily she'd forgotten the elderly woman's presence. "Oh, my lady, I do apologize for airing this in your hearing."

"No, no, my dear. I only wish I had someone to place a bet with about the outcome."

Audra could feel the floor quiver under her – though it must be only her knees trembling. "I beg you, my lady —"

"Not to pass along what I've heard today? Really, Audra dear, you underestimate me. Despite my carefully-cultivated reputation as an unrepentant gossip, when was the last time you heard me utter a juicy tidbit about anyone I like? And I do like your lively young charge here."

Dorinda said quietly, "Lord Kinley has never so much as *hinted…*"

It was far more likely, Audra thought, that Dorinda simply hadn't noticed.

"Of course he has not," Lady Stone said comfortably. "Such a possibility would never be discussed with a girl of your age."

"Not until the matter is entirely settled," Audra added, "to avoid prematurely raising the young woman's hopes."

Dorinda's eyes widened. "Then it's *not* arranged?"

Audra hesitated. "Melksham told me last night after dinner that he and Lord Kinley have come to an agreement. But I'm certain Lord Kinley will wait to make his formal offer out of respect for your feelings."

"*My* feelings?"

Audra could shake the girl. "Since he intends to live a quieter life, once married – as most gentlemen do, I must point out – he feels you deserve a full Season to enjoy yourself before settling down. I assure you this is a wonderful match. Lord Kinley is all that a young woman could hope for in a husband – a kind and gentle man."

Dorinda was still looking mulish.

Of all the gentlemen in the *ton*, Audra thought, how could the girl possibly find fault with Lucas? She played the trump card. "You'll be a countess, Dorinda. Think of the title – *my lady.*"

For a moment she thought Dorinda hadn't heard. Then the girl seemed to shake herself, and said quietly, "I shall think of nothing else."

How foolish, and how utterly predictable, that Dorinda would put a title above the more important aspects of a match, giving no thought to such things as her prospective husband's nature. But right now it hardly mattered. If Audra could just get Dorinda safely married, sooner or later the girl would surely come to appreciate Lucas's fine qualities and not just his title.

Audra turned to Lady Stone. "Thank you for everything, my lady – the party, your patience…"

Lady Stone gave a rusty laugh. "Don't mention it, Lady Audra. I found this morning's entertainment as good as a play. Do come back anytime!"

*****

They were only a few steps from Melksham House, so Audra passed the time by chatting about the weather and the sprigs of green starting to show in the garden at the center of Grosvenor Square, leaving serious discussion until they were safely behind closed doors.

But the moment the footman admitted them, Dorinda pleaded a headache and retreated to her room. She stayed there the rest of the day and asked for her dinner on a tray. After her own solitary meal, Audra went upstairs to confront her charge – but to her astonishment, Dorinda was dressed for Lord Pelham's ball. Her face was a bit pale, but she was as lovely as ever in a yellow dimity gown which made her red-blonde hair glow.

"I'm pleased to see you are recovered," Audra said.

"Yes, my lady."

"My dear, I must apologize. I should not have spoken of such matters, and especially not so suddenly. Of course you were taken aback."

Dorinda tilted her head, as if she were a great distance away and having trouble hearing. "No, I'm glad you said it, Lady Audra. You made me stop and think."

"I'm pleased to see you giving consideration to these important matters. A Season in London isn't *entirely* about having fun, you know."

"I have made up my mind to do whatever is necessary."

"I'm sure you'll find it is not such an onerous outcome. But in the meantime, there's no reason we can't enjoy tonight's ball. It's the last one, you know."

Dorinda's voice was a bare gasp. "Whatever do you mean – the last?"

"We have soirees to attend and musicales and the theater – oh, and a visit to the opera. But no more balls for a week or two, so we must make the most of this one. Come along now, for the carriage will be waiting."

They were fashionably late, and Audra half-expected Lucas would be there already – but he was nowhere in sight and she had to admit relief. If he wasn't present, then she didn't have to admit how her clumsiness had threatened to overset their bargain. Still, she kept the supper waltz for him as had become their custom, in case he appeared.

And he did – bowing before her just as the music started. "Dare I hope you were waiting for me, Lady Audra?"

"It's fortunate you're such a good dancer, or I would tell you I was already bespoken. I was beginning to think you preferred the company at your club."

"Impossible, when such a lively flirtation awaits me here."

Audra said too quickly, "I'm not flirting." *Am I? Surely not – I'm only having a good time with a friend.*

"I am corrected." Lucas swept her onto the floor.

But Audra was jittery and high-strung, and she knew her nerves would not settle until she had confessed. "I'm glad to have a moment with you before you see Dorinda. If she seems cool this evening, I hope you will not press her about why."

Lucas arched an eyebrow at her.

She fixed her gaze on the folds of his neckcloth because it was more comfortable than looking him in the eye. "I mentioned your plans for her future. I'm sorry, but after you and Melksham had your talk last night…"

"I ought to have known better than to trust Melksham's judgment."

Audra added hastily, "Dorinda was startled to hear the news, but she's fine now. She likes you a great deal. It's apparently just the marrying part she's not quite ready for. Perhaps you can reassure her you're willing to wait until she's accustomed to the idea."

He was silent as they circled the floor again.

Audra peeked up at him, noting the tightness of his jaw.

He drew a long breath. "You've no idea what a muck you've made of this, do you?"

She was stunned by the edge in his voice. Yes, she'd made a tactical error, but it wasn't like Lucas to hold an honest mistake against her.

The music ended and he guided her off the floor. "Come with me, Audra. There's a library where we can be private."

Was she to be marched off like a schoolgirl for a scold? "I assure you there's nothing you can say that I haven't already told myself. If you don't mind waiting until tomorrow to lambaste me, perhaps you and Melksham can take it in turns!" Despite her best efforts, her voice quavered.

A hesitant voice behind her said, "Lady Audra?"

Audra caught a glimpse of a brilliant scarlet coat. At the start of the evening, one of Dorinda's soldier friends had begged her for a country dance, and though Audra had tried to refuse, His Majesty's troops were persistent. Now she didn't know whether to be grateful for the interruption or annoyed that he must have heard her sharp words.

Lucas bowed and stepped away. Audra tried to smile. "Are you in the habit of rescuing damsels in distress, Captain?"

He looked alarmed. "Ma'am? How did you know about Dor… I mean… I don't understand."

Audra's eyes narrowed. "What were you going to say about Miss Grey?"

"Nothing, my lady. I…"

Audra ignored his stammer and let her gaze drift across the ballroom. No yellow dimity gown. No gleaming red-gold head. No Dorinda. She was probably in the ladies' withdrawing room, confiding in her friends. Unless…no, Audra could count all Dorinda's closest friends on the fringes of the room, waiting for the country dance to start. She beckoned one of them to her.

"Dorinda had a headache earlier," the girl said. "Perhaps she's lying down somewhere."

Lucas came up beside Audra, the annoyance gone from his voice. "What's wrong?"

Relief swept over her until she realized she would have to admit she had actually mislaid her brother's ward. "It's nothing. I'm sure Miss Grey will reappear at any moment."

Lucas turned to survey the crowd, then faced off with the scarlet-coated soldier. "Where's your friend? Andrews?"

"You mean James Andrews?" Audra asked with foreboding.

The soldier's face went the same shade as his coat. Lucas said something under his breath and left the ballroom. He came back a couple of minutes later, straight to Audra. "Melksham's carriage is gone, and Dorinda was seen getting into it with a young man in a red coat."

"Then she must be at home, but I don't understand why she allowed Captain Andrews to escort her rather than coming to me."

Because she didn't want to interrupt as you danced with Lucas, and flirted, and paid no attention to your charge. "Will you see me home, Lucas?" Her voice was very small.

A footman hailed a hackney for them, and Audra chewed her lip all the way to Grosvenor Square, trying not to think what she'd do if Dorinda wasn't there.

Lucas asked, "Where is Melksham tonight?"

"At his club, I think. He wasn't at home for dinner."

At Melksham House, the footman who opened the door said, "I haven't seen Miss Grey since you left for the ball, my lady."

"Have the duke's curricle sent around," Lucas ordered.

Audra gasped. "What are you doing?"

"Borrowing Melksham's pride and joy rather than wasting another half-hour going home to get my own rig." He sounded grim. "I'll find her, Audra, even if I have to chase her all the way to Scotland."

Audra turned to the footman. "Bring my heavy cloak, please."

"And where do you think you're going?" Lucas asked.

"With you, of course. Wherever Dorinda is, she must be chaperoned. You're not betrothed to her yet, so it's not fitting that you—"

"You're worried about how this looks?"

"Yes – and about what Melksham will say when he finds I've lost his ward."

"You don't want to face him, do you? Come along, if you insist, but it's going to be a cold ride. If you start to rip up at me about it, I may just stuff a fold of that cloak in your mouth to keep you quiet."

"You're threatening me with violence? At least I will be on hand to defend Dorinda from your rage if… *when* … we catch up with her."

"I would never rip up at Miss Grey," he said quietly.

Only at you. He might as well have said it. Audra winced. She deserved all the blame, yes – but if she lost his friendship because of her mistake, she would be devastated.

The horses pulled up in front of the house, stamping their hooves and blowing steam. "I'll take His Grace's driving coat as well," Lucas told the footman as he shed his own lighter wrap. A moment later, he handed Audra up into the curricle, gathered the reins, and nodded to the groom to let the team go.

The clatter of the hooves seemed to echo Audra's skittering heartbeats. If he was assigning no blame at all to Dorinda… "Do you think Captain Andrews has stolen her away?"

"*Stolen*—? Audra, what does it take for you to see what's directly under your nose? You announced to the girl that her future is set. What did you expect she'd do? Thank you for arranging her life?"

"Well – yes, I did. You believe she's eloped."

"So do you, for your suspicion was clear when I mentioned Captain Andrews. The question is why you believe it."

Audra said reluctantly, "She told me today she's convinced he is the man she wants. That's why I told her about you."

Lucas shook his head.

An hour into their drive, they stopped for fresh horses, and as they took the road again, Audra wrapped herself more tightly in her cloak. Lucas clucked to the team, and they sped down the moonlight-bathed road. "Why are you here, Audra? Why didn't you send for Melksham instead?"

"Because it's *our* lives which are hanging in the balance – Dorinda's, of course, but yours and mine too. Not Mellie's. He'll be furious if Dorinda ruins herself, but her actions won't destroy him. You and I, on the other hand, stand to lose everything."

"Yes," he said. "You and I. We need to talk about that."

But he seemed disinclined to go on, so Audra pulled her hood closer and blew on her fingers in an effort to stay warm.

A cloud bank covered the moon, and suddenly the road vanished. Lucas slowed the horses to a walk. Even without the wind whipping her face, Audra could barely feel her cheeks, and she swore her toes had turned to ice. Why hadn't she thought to change her dancing slippers for something warmer?

In the next village, Lucas pulled up in front of a small inn.

Audra jolted out of an uneasy doze. "Time to change horses again already?"

"It's too dark to go on and chance injuring an animal."

"But we must be close behind them."

"Not close enough," Lucas said wearily. He handed over the reins to Audra and climbed stiffly down to bang on the inn's door.

The landlord, when he finally came downstairs in his nightcap, was grumpy. "We're not a coaching inn, sir. For job horses, you need the Swan, in the next village."

"We require accommodation, that's all."

"We have no rooms made up."

"It's already the middle of the night," Lucas said reasonably. "If you can shelter the horses, we'll rest in one of your parlors and be on our way again at first light."

The landlord grumbled, but he called for his son to take the horses and stepped back from the door to let Lucas and Audra in.

"If you can provide the lady with tea, I'd be grateful," Lucas said.

Audra shivered as the landlord made up the fire in a tiny private parlor. Lucas paced the floor. A sleepy maid brought in a teapot, and Audra wrapped her hands around her cup and breathed in the steamy fragrance, hoping to thaw herself from the inside out. "Have some tea, Lucas. It helps."

He threw himself down on the settee next to her, and Audra filled a cup. "What are we going to do for money, by the way?" she asked. "I only have a few stray coins. If we don't catch up with her soon…" It would take days for them to get all the way to Scotland. What had she been thinking to leave home with nothing but the ball gown she was wearing?

Lucas grinned. "Fortunately, Melksham left a purse in his driving coat. I doubt he'll mind my borrowing it, since it's his ward we're trying to save."

"I'll reimburse him. It's not your fault the child's ruining her life." Audra's eyes brimmed with tears. "I'll never understand Dorinda. Why would she throw herself away on a soldier, when she could have *you*?"

Lucas went curiously still. "Careful, Audra, or I might get the foolish notion that you consider me a prize."

But you are. Audra shook her head in confusion.

"Well, there it is," Lucas said. "Please don't feel you need to explain any further."

"Surely you don't believe the financial straits your father created make you ineligible? At Lady Stone's ball, Miss Gardiner was making her feelings quite clear."

"I don't want Miss Gardiner. In any case, you put paid to that."

With Audra's plan to split her dowry, he meant – because after ignoring Miss Gardiner for weeks, he couldn't simply start courting the heiress again.

"I'm sorry about the money I promised you. Surely Mellie will let me…" But if Dorinda married her captain instead of a titled gentleman, Audra could no longer deliver on her promise to her brother – so the duke wouldn't have to honor his end of the bargain, either. Keeping her word to Lucas was impossible.

"Melksham's a cheery thought to top off the evening. Not only has his ward run away, but his sister is just about as thoroughly compromised as it's possible to be."

"Nonsense. I'm on the shelf."

"It would be amusing to see you try that argument out with your brother – if I wasn't the one who'll be facing his pistol while you dish out your Banbury tale."

"Yes, he'll rip up at me, but you can't think he'd challenge *you*! You're his ward's promised husband and I'm her chaperone. How could you possibly compromise me?"

Lucas turned to look at her. The firelight sparkled in his eyes and glinted in his dark hair. "Like this." His voice seemed to come from a distance. He cupped her chin, turned her toward him, and softly kissed her lips.

Audra froze. Something seemed to crack deep inside her, and suddenly she was clinging to Lucas, her arms almost convulsively tight around him.

"Shh," he murmured. "It's all right." He kissed her throat, her temple, the bridge of her nose, and then returned to her lips, nibbling and licking until the taste of him overwhelmed what little sense she still possessed and she opened her mouth because she wanted more. She was no longer chilly; everywhere he touched her, Audra prickled with heat. His fingertips traced the line of her throat down to the frill at the neckline of her low-cut ball gown, and she threw her head back to allow him easier access. He cupped her breast and she arched her back, pushing into his palm.

Eventually, he released her mouth and simply looked down at her, his eyes bright.

Dizzy, stunned by her wanton behavior, Audra remembered that he'd merely issued a teasing challenge; she'd done the rest.

"You do care for me," he whispered.

She could hardly deny it when her body was still quivering in abandon.

"Yes," Lucas mused, "I believe you're quite seriously compromised… but there's no need to explain this to Melksham. Marry me, Audra."

Audra felt ill. Had he simply turned her foolishness to his advantage? "You think we won't catch up with Dorinda in time, then. Do you need my dowry that badly? I promise – I'll manage to get the funds for you somehow. You don't have to lie to me."

He shook his head and said softly, "Your dowry, no. I need *you* that badly."

And I need you, Lucas.

She felt as though she'd been looking into a fogged mirror, but now the glass was clean and she could see every freckle of her reflection. This explained the gladness in her heart when she saw him again, and why she'd figured out how to peel him away from Miss Gardiner, and why she'd enjoyed conspiring with him as they danced and flirted.

This new realization even explained why she'd chosen to use Dorinda. It was because Audra had never quite believed in the success of her own scheme. No wonder she'd been confused and out of sorts when Lucas had spoken admiringly of her charge, and when he'd invited Dorinda to his home, and when he had approached Melksham with his offer…

The words burst out. "But you spoke to Melksham about Dorinda. He told me."

Lucas shook his head. "I talked to him about *you* – and he promised to let me approach you in my own way. Audra, I would never have offered for Dorinda."

"You led her on?" She was – illogically – both annoyed and relieved.

"Dorinda has considered me in the light of an uncle. It's a relationship I have carefully cultivated these past weeks. No wonder she panicked when you told her she was expected to marry me."

"But you agreed to my plan!"

"Of course I went along with your ridiculous scheme, because it allowed me to see you. To court you. To have what I've wanted for so long now."

"You were courting Miss Gardiner."

"You assumed I was courting her. But it was you I wanted, and you gave me the opening I needed."

Tears pooled in her eyes. "I can't take the chance, Lucas. Ask anyone in the *ton* – I'm a jinx. Offer to marry *The Poor Lamb*, and your lungs will turn to mush! First Alexander Shelburne and then Viscount Wornell… and then *you*."

"Alexander Shelburne got consumption, Audra. You barely knew him. How could that have been your fault?"

"But Wornell was my choice, and I loved him." *I thought it must be love, the way we struck angry sparks off each other.* "When he died, I believed the problem was that I cared for him."

"Because you'd had a schoolgirl fondness for Shelburne, too."

She nodded. "When you offered for me…"

"You accepted because you *didn't* care for me." He seemed very calm.

"I didn't think I did, because it felt so different. With you, everything was peaceful. Calm. *Right*." She sniffed, and he handed her a handkerchief. "Until you got pleurisy and could barely breathe. If I'd killed you too, Lucas, I couldn't have gone on living."

"Audra, unless it was your idea for Wornell to race his curricle to Bath in the middle of a snowstorm, you're no more to blame for his accident than you are for Shelburne's consumption. As for me, despite having pleurisy, I'm right here – and I'm still breathing."

"The important thing is that you're healthy – and that you remain so." She reached up to him, holding him close one last time, to give her the strength to give him up.

He nibbled the corner of her mouth and then kissed her long and deeply.

The parlor door opened, and the Duke of Melksham said, "What the devil are you two doing? I mean, of course, why are you here in this godforsaken village? It's perfectly clear what you're doing."

"Mellie!" Audra would have leaped to her feet, but Lucas was holding her too tightly. "How did you find us?"

"Saw my curricle parked all anyhow in front of the inn. Lucas, is this how you reward my longsuffering patience, by stealing my curricle and team? It was a long cold ride to catch up with you, only to find you tucked in and cozy."

Too late, Audra realized her hair was straggling down where Lucas had run his fingers through it, and her neckline was askew. "It's Dorinda we need to worry about, Mellie."

Melksham shook his head. "She's in London."

"No, she's not." Audra took a deep breath. "She's somewhere on her way to Scotland."

"What makes you say that?"

"Because I was a fool, and I frightened her – and she ran away from the ball. She took your carriage."

"Only as far as Lady Stone's, where she threw herself sobbing at my lady's feet, begging help so she didn't have to jaunt off to Gretna Green." Melksham shook his head. "Lady Stone dismissed the captain and sent for me, and I took Dorinda home."

"She really *is* at home?" Audra could hardly believe her ears.

"When I heard you'd gone running off with Lucas, muttering something about Scotland, I had the boys saddle a horse, and here I am." Melksham shed his second-best greatcoat. "Let me get a tankard of ale; I've a powerful thirst. Then you can tell me where you left my team, Lucas. I hope you remember."

The door creaked shut behind him, leaving a painful silence in the room. Audra wondered why she hadn't noticed light streaming in the window as dawn broke, and colored as she remembered exactly how they had passed the time.

"Mellie seems to be in a good mood, all things considered," she said. "And with Dorinda safe, I'm sure we can work it all out. My dowry, I mean." *You don't have to marry me after all.* She held her breath. Would Lucas seize the chance to escape?

"Remember when Melksham stopped pestering you to find a husband?"

"You said you told him to leave me alone."

"What I told him," Lucas said softly, "was that I still want to marry you. I never accepted your foolish determination to break off our betrothal, but instead of facing me, you sent that cold little note. By the time I was up and around again, you were gone – sealed away in Melksham's castle, refusing to see anyone. You're dangerous all right, Audra, but not in the way you think. If being in love with you was the problem, then I'd be choking to death right now after what we've been doing all night."

Melksham reappeared, tankard of ale in hand. "I'll pretend I didn't hear that. Show her the license, man – I'll wager it's been in your pocket since you picked it up."

Lucas didn't take his gaze off Audra's face as he pulled a sheet of parchment from his coat.

Audra stared at it, unbelieving. Her throat was so tight she could barely speak. "A special license? For us? You really did mean this to happen, all along?"

"In my mind I've been yours since last year. But if you're convinced that being betrothed to you is dangerous to my health, then let's not be betrothed. Let's get married – right now."

"What a capital notion," Melksham said. "Get it over with and then we can all go home." He drained his tankard. "I'll go find a priest, shall I? And another ale, while I'm at it."

The door closed gently behind him, but neither Lucas nor Audra paid any attention at all.

Her Wedding Wager

Wednesday

The invitation for Celia to join Lady Stone's house party arrived at midday, and the few hours from then until the family sat down to dinner were the happiest Celia could ever remember. She was so absorbed in sorting out which gowns she would take, and her maid was so occupied with laying them gently into Celia's trunks, that they both forgot about dinner until the gong sounded.

Though Celia scrambled into the nearest frock and rushed downstairs, she found the parlor empty. She considered tiptoeing back up to her room and asking her maid to bring her a tray – but she couldn't honorably expect her mother to make excuses to Uncle Rupert for a wayward daughter. So Celia took her courage in both hands and strolled into the dining room, where the footmen had already started to serve the soup.

She'd been foolish to hope she could slip into her chair without being noticed. Her mother whimpered as Uncle Rupert's tight-browed glare came to rest on Celia. To make matters worse, directly across from Celia's customary place sat her cousin Simon, present at the family table for the first time in a full week. The moment she appeared, he rose and flourished a bow in her direction.

Of all the times for Simon Montrose to remember his manners. Celia couldn't recall the last occasion when he'd treated her so politely, and of course now he'd done it only to draw attention to her gaffe. She could tell by the dimple which only appeared in his left cheek when he thought he'd got the best of her.

"I'm sorry to be late, Mama. Beg pardon, Uncle Rupert." She sank into the chair the footman held, unfolded her napkin, and cast a limpid look across the table at Simon. "Thank providence our guest is–" *Nobody important. "* –only family."

Simon Montrose's gaze flicked over her. "Fortunate for you, Silly, that there was no need to make yourself presentable this evening."

Celia felt color surge into her cheeks. He needn't be rude, even if the frock she'd so hastily seized was one she hadn't worn since last year – when she'd still been in the schoolroom and her figure hadn't been quite so developed. And to use that dreadful nickname, too – the one he'd invented when she was six and he was ten, on the very day they'd met for the first time. Both families had been visiting Uncle Rupert…

Let slip how much it annoys you, and he'll never call you anything else. "Uncle, did Mama tell you of my good fortune?"

"She had just informed me that you felt unwell. Yet here you are, all smiles."

Celia tried not to grimace. Mrs. Overton's nerves made her hopeless at telling the smallest of social fibs, but she must not have considered the consequences of a tale like that. If Celia was truly unwell tonight, she could hardly hop into a carriage tomorrow to ride off cross-country to a party.

Uncle Rupert tasted his soup and pushed the dish aside, with a curt gesture to the butler to bring the next course. "I suppose by *good fortune*, you're referring to this fandango about some festivity or other."

"Yes, Uncle. Lady Stone has invited me to join her house party. It's a wonderful opportunity, for she–"

"Lady Stone. That meddling old gossip we met last year in Tunbridge Wells?"

Celia took a deep breath. "That wasn't at all what I was going to say, Uncle. She's invited a group of young people to a house party to celebrate the wedding of her niece, and she's being so kind as to introduce me to them."

"Young men, you mean," Rupert said repressively.

Mrs. Overton looked taken aback. "But of course, Rupert. How is Celia ever to marry, if she doesn't meet suitable young men? It is so kind of her ladyship to act as a sort of fairy godmother and include our girl. And at a wedding, too! – It's magical how such an event turns a gentleman's thoughts to his own future. I understand Lady Stone's nephew will be there – he holds the title now, you know. And she mentioned a viscount, as well as a baron or perhaps two."

Celia cut gently across the guest list. "Mama's right, Uncle. How else am I to meet eligible men? Since you are reluctant for me to have a Season in London…"

He snorted. "Waste my blunt on frills and fripperies and the hire price for a house in the City, when the London swells would see only that you're the great-niece of a tradesman? I think not."

The *ton* would be more likely to view Uncle Rupert as a vulgar mushroom than as a mere tradesman, for the one indisputable fact about Rupert Overton was that his ventures into trade had made him astonishingly rich.

"That is true," Celia said quietly. "But I'm also the granddaughter of a baron."

"Coming over all hoity-toity about it, are we? I've not noticed the connection to a title doing either you or your mother any good these last twenty years, missy."

Celia had to admit Uncle Rupert had a point. The baron who had sired Celia's mother had disowned his daughter when she married into a family which made and sold cloth – and so far as Celia knew, Mrs. Overton had never heard so much as a word from her family since.

Noting the way her mother's lower lip trembled at the reminder, Celia changed the subject. "As I was about to say, Uncle Rupert, if a London Season is out of the question, then Lady Stone's house party is by far your best opportunity to get me off your hands and married. You keep telling me that the young men I meet at the assemblies here are far beneath my touch."

"And so they are. Haven't seen any yet with ambition or good sense. And not a one with so much as a pair of coppers to rub together, either, which is why they cast their gaze toward my fortune. But the only man you need is right here." Rupert waved his fork toward Simon.

Her cousin? Of course he wasn't serious, to imply that she and *Simon*...

Celia couldn't help it. She giggled.

The dining room went silent. The butler, who was pouring her wine, seemed to freeze. Not even the clink of a spoon broke the spell.

Celia's gaze slid toward Simon. For a moment, she thought he looked annoyed – but then he gathered his customary calm and helped himself to pheasant from the platter the footman offered.

Finally Rupert spoke. "Find the idea amusing, do you, that you're to marry Simon?"

Celia cleared her throat. "Well, yes, I do. I mean, you've hinted it often enough, sir, but you can't possibly be serious."

"And why is that?" Rupert's tone was ominous.

"It's the sort of arrangement that must have seemed logical when we were children – keeping the family money all in a lump, and so on. But as it turns out, we simply don't suit." She sent a look across the table at Simon, pleading. "Tell him!"

Simon cut a bite of pheasant. "I confess, Uncle, this is one of a mere handful of occasions in my life when I find myself in complete agreement with my cousin. I can think of no option less inviting at present."

Celia's mouth dropped open. *I didn't ask you to make me sound like an antidote!*

"Considering your options, are you, my boy? Would one of those options be Lady Hester Billings?" Rupert said shrewdly. "Oh yes – I know you've been nibbling round the manor house, entertaining yourself with the earl's daughter. You'd better be cautious there."

A flicker of color rose in Simon's lean cheeks.

"Lady Hester?" Celia said. "Simon, are you daft? Lady Hester would *never* —"

"No more daft than you, Silly – thinking you can snap up a title in a few days at a party."

"Children," Mrs. Overton protested faintly.

"Oh, yes," Rupert murmured, "*now* I see evidence of the strain of blue blood each of you sports. A sharp tongue and a sense of being better than your fellows – those qualities must have come from the titled sides of your respective parentages, for they surely didn't arise in the Overtons."

Hair stirred on Celia's nape. Rupert, she had long ago learned, was most dangerous when he turned to sarcasm.

Mrs. Overton fluttered a small, plump hand. "But that's only because you've never been in a position to get to know these people, Rupert." Celia winced and tried to catch her mother's eye, but Mrs. Overton carried straight on. "I have. And I'm persuaded Lady Stone will present only suitable young men from excellent families, ones who are worthy of my beautiful Celia."

"Titled idlers with nothing to do but drink and gamble away their days and nights! You're not doing your daughter's cause any good, ma'am. I'm of a mind to forbid her going."

Celia wanted to melt into a puddle and sob, but she knew better than to show weakness. "Uncle, it would be too rude of me to refuse the invitation now. The guests are to begin gathering tomorrow, and the wedding is next week. Surely it can do no harm for me to meet new people."

"You'll send word to her meddlesome ladyship that your plans have changed, and you and Simon will start planning *your* wedding."

Simon said quietly, "No, Uncle Rupert. We won't. You cannot dictate who we marry – neither Celia nor I – nor when."

Relief flooded through her. Simon had stood up for her – had *defended* her! For a moment she stared at him in wonder, even fancying that the candlelight falling on his dark hair glittered like the helm of a knight of old.

She caught his eye and smiled, hoping he would read her apology in her expression. Lady Hester wasn't such a bad sort, really. A young woman in her position was bound to be overly fond of herself. And she was reasonably pretty. A man who found Lady Hester appealing wasn't *necessarily* daft, especially if one considered the business contacts which could rise out of such an acquaintance. Just as long as Simon didn't let himself believe that the daughter of an earl might actually marry a nobody.

Rupert ate his roast mutton in complete silence, as if he hadn't heard Simon's declaration. Even Mrs. Overton seemed to belatedly realize speaking wasn't safe.

When at length the plates were removed and the sweet brought in, Rupert said, "'Tis true I cannot force you to stand at the altar and take vows. But neither can you expect me to admire or support this quest. If you believe that in only a few days you can capture a title — "

Celia said lightly, "Every girl dreams of being a duchess, Uncle, but I'm only hoping to meet a pleasant, gentle man. Someone I could grow fond of."

She didn't realize she'd let her gaze rest on Simon until he raised a cynical eyebrow at her. "In contrast to present company, you mean?"

"You needn't take it personally. I wasn't talking about you." *Not exactly, anyway.*

Rupert cleared his throat. "If the time comes when this *pleasant, gentle man* of yours asks what you will bring him as a dowry, Celia, don't count on me to step up with an offer."

Mrs. Overton gasped. "You cannot mean you would disown your niece, sir?"

"Celia is the one who disowns her flesh and blood – the family which raised her, fed her, and schooled her – when she announces that only among the aristocracy can she can find a man who suits her."

Celia suspected that pointing out the lapses in Uncle Rupert's logic would be as fruitless as trying to explain her meaning to Simon.

Rupert's gaze came to rest on her so intently that Celia wondered for a moment if she had a bit of haricots verts stuck between her front teeth. "You maintain that you can return from this visit betrothed to a gentleman who carries a title?"

Celia opened her mouth to argue that she'd said no such thing. Honestly, if Uncle Rupert was going to get his nose out of joint, couldn't he at least take care to get the details correct?

She understood her uncle's ire, of course; he was offended that the two young people under his guardianship had both so firmly – and perhaps not very politely – put paid to his long-held notion of creating an Overton family dynasty.

Across the table, Simon said mildly, "You know, it *did* sound as if that's what you expect to happen, Silly. You show yourself at the wedding, the men fall into line, and you select one as easily as you just chose the apricot tart over the trifle."

Celia glared at him. "You're a fine one to talk, Simon. I suppose you believe all you need do is declare yourself and Lady Hester will start to assemble her trousseau."

"We were not discussing me. Would you care to make a wager on your chances?"

Mrs. Overton's eyes grew round. "Really, Simon dear, you cannot *wager* on such things!"

"I don't see why he shouldn't," Rupert said, "if he's willing to take the risk. Celia seems very certain of herself. Perhaps you could fund your dowry with your winnings, miss, since I'm not willing to do so – as long as the stake Simon offers is high enough to satisfy your fancy husband."

Celia finally managed to get her voice back. "I suppose if I'm not willing to accept the wager, Uncle, you expect I shall give up the house party, stay here, and marry Simon?"

"*Not* an option, Silly," Simon murmured. "I think you've hoisted yourself pretty far up your own petard."

"Believe me, I wasn't considering the possibility. I was only asking whether Uncle Rupert has withdrawn his objection to me going to the party."

Rupert said judiciously, "It would hardly be fair of me not to allow you the sporting chance to win the funds for your dowry."

Simon frowned. "I wasn't thinking of dowry-sized stakes, Uncle."

"Oh?" Celia mocked. "Perhaps you're having second thoughts about the wisdom of offering a wager?" *Stop it. You'd have to be a lunatic to bet with him. Just pretend he didn't say it – any of it.*

"Oh, I'll win – but I want to be assured you can pay me. How far can you make your pin money stretch?"

The butler brought in the port, and Mrs. Overton stood up. "This discussion is finished. Celia, we are leaving the gentlemen. *Now.*"

Celia rose reluctantly to follow her mother.

"I'll consider throwing in an apology if you pull off the scheme," Simon added. "A public apology for thinking you couldn't do it."

"Now that," Celia snapped, "is an incentive I'd find difficult to refuse!" She stormed out to follow her mother down the long and drafty hall to the drawing room.

Mrs. Overton sank onto a settee, gasping for air and fanning herself. "Oh, Celia, my pet, what were you thinking?"

"I'm so sorry, Mama. I know better than to let Simon get my goat."

"I wasn't speaking of Simon. Oh, it's true that teasing you with a foolish wager was not well-done of him, but he's a harmless boy, really. It's your Uncle Rupert who worries me. Speaking to him that way… Celia, my dear, if he were to disown you—"

"Don't be absurd, Mama. If I should return home betrothed to a titled gentleman, Uncle Rupert would immediately find a way to turn the connection to his advantage. And if I don't – well, he'd hardly throw me out of the house, for he'd find too much enjoyment in reminding me how I'd failed."

"But Celia, you can't simply disobey him!" Mrs. Overton's voice cracked. "He might truly disown you, and then what about me? To your uncle, I've always been just the inconvenient widow of his nephew. He tolerates me only for your sake."

"Nonsense, Mama. What would he do without you to run his house?"

"Hire a housekeeper," Mrs. Overton said tartly.

"I'm persuaded he would not part with the coin to do so."

But Mrs. Overton was not mollified. "I feel shame to admit it, but I have always relied on your prospects, Celia. It has been a comfort to know that when your uncle goes, you will be well-enough provided for that I could have a cottage somewhere and..."

"Of course I will look after you, Mama." Celia stopped abruptly. How many times over the years had she made that sort of blithe promise? But now...

"What if he refuses to allow you to attend this wedding?"

"Then I'll go anyway – even if I have to sneak out."

"Celia! If you defy his wishes—"

"Mama! Are you saying you believe I shouldn't go after all?"

Mrs. Overton burst into tears. "If you displease him—"

"But Mama, if I surrender to this ... this blackmail of his, there will be no end. Any time Uncle Rupert wished to bring me to heel, he would merely have to threaten to disown me – and what could I do? If I give up this opportunity and next week he once more determines that my cousin and I should be wed—"

"Well, if it comes to that, Simon would hardly be the *worst*..." Mrs. Overton gulped when Celia glared at her, and sputtered on. "But you know best, my dear, and if you truly believe that the two of you should not suit, then of course this wedding party is the most promising chance of making a suitable match. But what if you're not successful there?"

Warily, Celia eyed her mother. "We'll discuss it in the morning." She rang the bell for her mother's maid. "Perhaps an early bed tonight, Mama? Things will look better when the sun is shining."

At least, she hoped so – but suddenly Simon's wager of mere money was a trifling thing indeed, a mere distraction from the true issue. What Celia had really staked on this house party, it appeared, was her entire future – and her mother's.

*****

When Simon left Uncle Rupert to his account books and went to join the ladies, he found Celia sitting alone by the fire in the quiet drawing room. For a moment when Simon noted the droop of her shoulders, he felt almost sorry for her. She looked more like the child she'd once been – thin and small, with ordinary brown hair and dark blue eyes far too big for her face – than the young lady she'd grown into. The *prickly* young lady. That much was his fault, no doubt, because she'd always been far too much fun to tease. Not that she hadn't repaid the favor from time to time.

She sat up straight as he came in. "I'll ring for the coffee tray." She turned with a determined smile which lasted only a moment. "Oh. It's only you."

"No coffee for me, thank you. I came in to tell you Uncle Rupert has gone to his book room to finish up paperwork."

"And Mother's gone to bed." She nibbled her lower lip. "Tell me honestly, Simon. Do you think I should give up the house party? Send my regrets to Lady Stone and miss the wedding?"

"Hell, no."

"Don't pussyfoot about hurting my feelings!" She shuddered. "I'm afraid if I don't stand up to Uncle on this matter, we're likely to find ourselves at the altar before Christmas."

"He seems to have entirely forgotten that he was initially opposed to your going."

"Really?" Her eyes brightened. "He won't stand in my way?"

"It seems not. It was brilliant of you to make it a sporting event."

"I can hardly take credit for you proposing a wager – but if it accomplishes my purpose, I suppose I must be grateful for your suggestion."

"That reminds, me, Silly – we never set the stakes."

She shrugged. "Fifty guineas?"

"That's hardly worth the bother. What happened to your confidence? Of course, you're putting a lot of faith in this so-called fairy godmother. What if she turns out to be a witch instead?"

She tipped her head to one side. "You should want me to win, Simon, because my victory will set you free too. If I lose, Uncle Rupert will redouble his efforts to marry us off to each other. Very well – let's make it five hundred. That's a small price to pay for your freedom."

"That sum should be enough to keep your mind focused," he said dryly. "Done."

She held out her hand. "And don't forget the public apology."

"I said I'd consider it. The real prize you stand to win isn't my money, anyway. It's a title and a country estate and a life of ease. And the gentleman who provides all of those things. We must hope you can find one who retains his hair and a reasonable number of teeth." He felt unholy glee at the way her eyes sparked; it was a good thing his cravat wasn't flammable, or her gaze would have set him afire.

She rose stiffly. "I will retire now, as I have to finish packing."

"Uncle Rupert has agreed to send you in the carriage tomorrow, by the way, instead of making you pay for a post-chaise out of your pin money." Simon shot a sideways look at her and added airily, "He insists that I go with you."

Her fingers trembled, reminding him that he was still holding her hand. "What? Why?"

"To protect you on the road, he said, but I think his real intention is for me to get a look at your prospective suitors and report back to him. I must be off to my lodgings. We will need to make an early start of it."

He couldn't help whistling as he left the room – because the expression on her face really was priceless.

Thursday

Though Uncle Rupert's carriage was nothing fancy to look at, it was well-sprung and the horses Simon selected at the various coaching inns were mostly lively. The roads had been baked hard by the summer's heat, and autumn rains would not begin for another month at least. So they arrived at Lady Stone's country home, a sprawling Jacobean manor located on a hilltop overlooking a Derbyshire valley, in good time.

"Lady Stone is in the drawing room," the butler intoned, showing them the way.

A beady-eyed old woman, tall and thin and with a nose which would have looked right at home on a hunting hawk, was drinking port by the fire. She waved them into the room. "Welcome to Rockhill House. Not my idea to name it that, of course – some fool in a previous generation of Stones enjoyed puns."

Celia had all she could do not to look at Simon, but she was fairly sure seeing the gleam of appreciation in his eyes would set her off into uncontrollable giggles. Then she remembered she was still annoyed at him, so she concentrated on their hostess instead. "It's a lovely house, Lady Stone. But if you dislike the name, why have you not changed it?"

"My stubborn fool of a husband refused, because it had been in his family for three hundred years. Now his nephew – the current Lord Stone – turns out to be just as set in his ways as the last earl ever was." Lady Stone eyed Simon with appreciation, sparing barely a glance at Celia. "Tell me, Celia dear – who is this delectable young man you've brought?"

Delectable? Celia almost turned her head to check whether someone had swapped out Simon for another male while she wasn't watching. "My mother felt it necessary to remain with my uncle, and my cousin was dispatched to make certain all was well on the road. May I present Simon Montrose?"

Simon bowed gracefully. "I am honored, my lady – and devastated that I missed meeting you last year at Tunbridge Wells. With my uncle gone to take the waters for his health, I was needed to run his business."

"Montrose," Lady Stone mused. "I used to know a family of that name, long ago. Or perhaps I'm thinking of a title. My lamentable memory."

"It was both, I believe," Simon murmured. "Regrettably, I'm only a distant cousin of those Montroses, ma'am."

Lady Stone's beady gaze swept him from head to foot once more. "Of course you'll stay for the house party, Mr. Montrose. You have arrived just as I realized I need an extra man, and when fate presents such a modest and charming individual, I cannot resist. Also, I'm afraid the young ladies would have my ears if I allowed you to leave."

Modest? Charming? Celia wanted to growl, but she kept her voice level. "Simon can't possibly remain, my lady, for he's far too busy with his responsibilities. At least to hear him tell it, our Uncle Rupert could not get through a day without him."

Lady Stone hadn't taken her gaze off Simon. "That would be Mr. Rupert Overton? I believe when we first met, Celia told me he's in the cloth-manufacturing business."

"He used to be," Simon said easily. "Now he's more involved in arranging capital for people who wish to be in the cloth-manufacturing business. I help him decide which investments are most worthwhile, and match those who have money to invest with those who have plans."

"So in effect you're a banker? Some of my favorite acquaintances are bankers. Just think of how you could expand Mr. Overton's business among the people you'll meet here. There's my own nephew, for instance – my late husband left him swimming in lard and without any idea of what to do with it all. His idea of investing is simply medieval. You'll meet him at dinner, Celia dear."

Celia, who had felt almost invisible for the last few minutes, stumbled over her answer.

"And my niece's betrothed, Lord Tavish, is full of juice as well, though he may not be quite in the mood to discuss investments this week." Lady Stone reached for a bell on the table beside her and rang it sharply. "My companion will take you to your rooms and get you settled. Oh, where is that girl? Jane!"

A moment later, a young woman in a plain dark blue dress came into the room.

As Lady Stone began to give instructions, Celia leaned toward Simon. "You *can't* stay."

"Why shouldn't I? My pedigree is every bit as good as yours. Or as bad, depending on how you look at it."

Until Lady Stone's vague recollection of a title, Celia had almost forgotten that Simon's great-grandfather – or was it two greats? – had been a viscount. Like the baron who was technically Celia's grandfather, that particular long-dead ancestor had never been a subject for discussion in the Overton household. She had no trouble believing Simon's genealogy right now, however, for he wore an expression as arrogant as any earl or duke could command.

Celia tried again. "Last night you made it quite clear you're not putting yourself in parson's mousetrap anytime soon."

"But how often will I get such a wonderful opportunity – fairy godmother and all?"

She could hardly argue that point when she was pinning her own hopes on these few days, so Celia cast round for other objections. "You haven't any suitable clothes with you."

"I brought a few things so I could go on to Bradford to complete some business. It's a small matter to dispatch a messenger for what I'll need."

"But you must be anxious to get home." *To Hester*, she almost added.

He smiled. "If you're enjoying the thought of a few days away from Uncle Rupert, imagine my relief at having such a wonderful excuse to stay away."

"Excuse? You're never going to tell him you seized the chance to find a titled bride!"

"Oh, no. Uncle will agree with Lady Stone about the contacts I could make here – so long as he doesn't realize it was her idea."

In desperation, Celia played her last card. "Surely Lady Hester would not be pleased to hear that you leaped at the chance to attend a house party full of young ladies." *And she'll find out, even if I have to tell her myself.*

"You assured me last night Lady Hester is a waste of my time, and I could not possibly ignore your sage advice. I'm looking forward to meeting the young ladies."

That was a clanker, but clearly Celia had lost this round. She smiled and murmured, "I shall make certain to give you every assistance in that regard."

Lady Stone said, "Jane, dear, instruct the housekeeper that Mr. Montrose is to be added to the party. She can put him in the green room." She turned around. "Celia, did I hear you mention Lady Hester Billings?"

Embarrassed at having been caught whispering behind their hostess's back, Celia reluctantly admitted, "Yes, ma'am."

"What a lovely happenstance, for she's one of the bridesmaids. I'm sure she'll be delighted to see you again – both of you." Lady Stone smiled broadly.

Simon looked disconcerted at that news, and Celia made a mental note to pay particular attention when the two came face to face.

Lady Stone's companion was a pleasant, businesslike young woman only a couple of years older than Celia, and she didn't even give a long-suffering sigh over her assignment. Perhaps, Celia thought, that was because Jane was busy admiring Simon's profile – and his other assets – as she took them through the manor house and up the stairs. The companion paused at the intersection of two long corridors and indicated a door.

"Here is the green room, Mr. Montrose. I'm certain Miss Overton's trunks have already been brought upstairs, but I'll check on your luggage."

"I stuffed a few things in my saddlebags," Simon said carelessly. "Perhaps I can get the bootboy to run to the stables and retrieve them for me."

Celia thought the companion had to suppress a shudder at the idea of a gentleman's clothing being so carelessly handled. "I shall arrange for one of the footmen to act as your valet, sir." Jane took a step back and ran her gaze over him – with perhaps not quite so much admiration as she'd displayed earlier, Celia noted. "Thomas may be able to arrange a loan of the things you'll need."

"I'm certain I can manage with what I brought," Simon murmured.

"Gentlemen always dress for dinner at Rockhill," Jane warned, and then apparently decided to leave that battle for the footman. "Miss Overton, you'll be in the lavender room, just this way."

As they strolled on down the quieter of the two corridors, Jane eyed her. "Is your cousin really as much of a rough diamond as he seems?"

"Worse," Celia said.

But it might be amusing to take Simon at his word where the young ladies were concerned. It would be a bit of a challenge to draw their attention to him, of course. Simon was Simon, after all. But if there was a swarm of young women pestering her cousin, he'd have to leave Celia alone while he fended them off.

She might as well start right away. "But despite his unkempt edges, he truly is a gentleman." *At least, he can act like one when he tries.*

Two young women came out of a nearby bedroom and stopped to inspect Celia. Jane said, "Miss Prudence Carew, and Miss Dimity Carew, may I present Miss Overton?"

The sisters bobbed tiny curtsies. "Oh, yes," one of them said. "Lady Stone told us you were coming. Your uncle is the cotton-weaver."

"Dimity," her sister warned.

Celia smiled. "Not quite, though he owns a few factories where others weave cotton – often into fabric just as fine as what you're wearing."

"Oh, well," Dimity said with a shrug. "It's very much the same thing. Jane, what was Lady Stone thinking? But then of course, she hired *you*, so I suppose we can't expect—"

"Come along, Dimity. We'll be late for the rehearsal." Her sister tugged Dimity along the corridor and out of sight.

Celia noted the slight flush which had risen in Jane's cheeks and didn't bother to keep the edge of sarcasm out of her voice. "*Charming* young ladies."

Jane smiled and continued down the corridor to a tall, heavy door. "Unfortunately for you, you'll be just next door to them. They're sharing a room so they can chaperone each other."

Inside the lavender bedroom, Celia's maid was unpacking the trunks, exclaiming over the way dresses had shifted and creased as they traveled.

"If you need anything at all," Jane said, "the housekeeper will be happy to help. Or come to find me. I'm at the end of this corridor on the left. Dinner is at eight; I'll come and fetch you tonight so you don't have to walk in alone."

*****

When Celia saw the gauntlet which waited for her in the drawing room a few minutes before eight o'clock, she was grateful to have Jane at her side.

They were apparently the last to appear, and the silence stretched out as everyone in the drawing room paused to study Celia. The assessing looks seemed to analyze her pale blue gown, the wealth of chestnut hair piled atop her head, her mother's strand of pearls, her dainty shoes, her delicate Brussels-lace fan. The Carew sisters looked disgruntled – perhaps because they couldn't find fault with her. Celia was once more grateful that despite her years of living retired from the *ton*, Mrs. Overton had maintained a lively sense of both fashion and good taste.

The two Miss Carews were decked out in perfect imitation of the virginal debutante. Each wore flowing white muslin trimmed with satin ribbons – one dress accented in yellow, the other in pink. The dresses were simple enough, but Celia, as the niece of a former cloth merchant, knew quite well that fabric so fine and delicate would have cost very nearly as much as silk.

Lady Hester, apparently released from the rule of wearing pastels because she had already finished her first Season, was dressed in a lush dark green fabric that draped around her as intimately as a whisper. Her hair was arranged in an artfully-tangled coiffure which made it look to Celia as if she'd just gotten out of bed. The bride, Lady Stone announced, was dining with the family of her betrothed, at their estate nearby.

As for the gentlemen, Celia thought she recognized a modified version of Lady Stone's beaky nose. She had nearly decided that the unfortunate man attached to it must be Lord Stone until she remembered that the new peer must have been related to Lady Stone's husband instead. So he couldn't have inherited her nose.

There were also a couple of younger men, one of whom had a hairstyle as elegantly messy as Lady Hester's. Celia looked past the two of them and her gaze caught on Simon, who appeared refreshingly normal in comparison.

He was the tallest of the gentlemen, and his raiment was the simplest, with only a fanciful bit of embroidery on his waistcoat relieving the stark contrast of black coat and white linen. If that was a borrowed set of evening clothes, Celia concluded, the footman pressed into service as his makeshift valet must be very skilled indeed.

Lady Stone raised her glass. "Now our little party is complete, and we all have nothing to do for the next few days but have fun and get Imogene safely married. Come here, Celia, and let me introduce you."

Though the drawing room had seemed crammed with people, by the time the dinner gong sounded a few minutes later, Celia thought she had everyone straight. The gentleman with the beaky nose was Lord Lockwood, and the one with the messy hair was Baron Draycott. It turned out that Lord Stone had been standing off in a corner wearing an abstracted air. In fact, he looked as though he wasn't quite certain what all these people were doing in his house, much less whether he was supposed to be enjoying himself. The last gentleman, Celia recognized when she took a closer look; though she'd never been face to face with him before, everyone in the neighborhood knew Lady Hester's brother, Viscount Billings.

"We're going to ignore etiquette rules," Lady Stone said cheerfully. "Jane has it all planned so at dinner each evening, you'll be matched with different partners. Line everyone up, my dear."

Celia found herself partnered with Lord Lockwood. Close up, he was clearly the oldest of the party – she'd guess he was at least forty, and as he bowed before her, she noticed the patches where his scalp showed pink through his thinning mousy-brown hair. Simon appeared to be taking note as well; he caught her eye and shook his head a fraction. She remembered him saying, *We must hope that he retains his hair and a reasonable number of teeth,* and clenched her jaw as she laid her hand on Lord Lockwood's sleeve.

The corner of Simon's mouth twitched as he offered his arm to one of the Carew sisters – who seemed not to see him. "My lady," she whined. "I thought you said I could..."

Lady Stone cut the girl off before she could finish her sentence. "Nonsense, Dimity. You should have been taught to take turns and share your toys years ago."

Celia couldn't quite smother a smile at the idea that Simon was going to get exactly what he deserved for pushing himself into the party – being condemned to spend a couple of hours in company with that young woman.

"You look quite pleased with your circumstances, Miss Overton," Lady Hester cooed under her breath as she laid her hand on Baron Draycott's arm. "Though perhaps you shouldn't be. Lady Stone is so fair-minded. Why, it's almost as though she were handicapping a horse race by giving a head start to the very weakest runners."

*****

Miss Carew eventually unbent and began speaking to him, though Simon didn't fool himself that she had suddenly found him charming. Perhaps she was too bored to be silent any longer. He was relieved when Lady Stone finally signaled the end of dinner and the ladies withdrew, leaving the gentlemen to their port.

The butler set the decanters on the table, cleared the last of the crumbs, and departed. Across the table Baron Draycott leaned forward on his elbows and said confidentially, "Did I hear Lady Stone say Miss Overton is a close relation of yours, Montrose?"

"A cousin, yes, but not very close. We have a great-uncle in common, no more."

Draycott nodded. "Ah. That would be the weaver, I suppose?"

Simon tried not to show his annoyance.

"Don't fly off into the boughs," the baron said quickly. "I admire a man who can make something of himself. Especially when it lets him fund a dowry for a girl as pretty as that one."

Pretty? Yes, Simon supposed Celia was generally considered to be pretty, now that she'd grown up. At least, the young men back in Leicester seemed of one mind in considering her to be more than acceptable. Simon's own tastes ran more toward Lady Hester's style of dark and exotic beauty, but he prided himself on being fair-minded about it. Celia's skin was gloriously smooth and soft – the perfect peaches and cream that every English girl longed for. Her features were regular, her smile could be delightful, and her hair had somehow turned from the ordinary brown of her childhood to something that looked gold or red or something else entirely, depending on the light.

As though he'd read Simon's mind, Draycott mused, "I wonder how long her hair is. And what do the ladies call that color?"

"No idea." Celia complained sometimes about how heavy it was, and Simon supposed it must be a nuisance, piled on top of her head like that. Back before she'd become a proper young lady, Celia's hair had flowed well past the middle of her back – though she'd usually worn it in two lush, fat, long braids which had fairly begged to be tugged.

"She's presentable enough, too," the baron went on. "Has a pleasant manner, doesn't put on airs or thrust herself forward. There's no sense in *me* marrying someone who expects to be treated like a duchess, for it won't happen."

Not if it depends on her husband acting like a gentleman.

"Of course, there's nothing wrong with being a baroness," Draycott went on defensively. "The title was good enough for my mother. It's just that some girls are too high in the instep to settle for what they consider a minor title. Lady Hester gave me quite a set-down just this afternoon, in fact, and all I'd said was … well, it doesn't matter. A gentleman doesn't gossip where ladies are concerned."

"Indeed," Simon murmured.

"Oh, yes. No sense in you looking in that direction, either – Lady Hester, I mean – since you've no title at all. I was just saying it stands to reason that Miss Overton would be more understanding about the matter. Granddaughter of a baron herself, I believe Lady Stone said? She'd no doubt be flattered if I offered for her."

Simon couldn't stop gritting his teeth long enough to answer, though he wasn't quite certain why. Surely he wasn't feeling grim for Celia's sake, or worried about her future – even though this little worm of a baron seemed to shop for a wife with less concern than he'd spend on choosing a new coat from his tailor.

His reaction must be because Celia was apparently already well on the way to winning her bet. Draycott might hold only the lowest of the nobility's ranks, but he did fit the terms of her wager. Why hadn't Simon been more careful to specify what it would take for her to win?

The baron went on hastily, "Not saying I *will* drop my handkerchief there, so don't you go running off to tell her, mind!"

"Of course not." Simon let a faint note of irony creep into his voice. "A gentleman doesn't gossip where ladies are concerned."

"What? Oh, you're mocking me. Very amusing. At any rate, there's plenty of time. Nearly an entire week."

"Yes," Simon said maliciously. "Only a fool wouldn't be able to make a determination in four or five days whether a female was the sort one wanted to spend a lifetime with."

Draycott nodded. "Exactly. And even if Lady Hester is unavailable, there are still the Carew sisters to consider."

Simon wondered if the baron saw any distinction between the two Carews. If it wasn't for the different colors of their ribbons, he wasn't certain he himself could tell them apart. "Still in the running for your hand, are they?"

"Well, of course. One of the richest families in the country."

"Lady Stone said their grandfather is an earl?"

"True, but they don't have the same airs and graces about it that Lady Hester puts on. Much more down to earth. Take the dresses they're wearing tonight, for example – they're so practical they're almost plain. A man could grow fond of a female with such simple tastes."

Simon bit his tongue to keep from enlightening the baron about the cost per bolt of that particular grade of muslin. The man probably wouldn't believe him anyway.

Draycott leaned closer. "Just between you and me, old chap – what's Miss Overton's dowry like?"

At the moment? Non-existent. Simon refilled his port glass. "A bit premature to start that investigation before you even know whether you're interested."

"Nonsense. Of course Lady Stone wouldn't include any girl who didn't have a respectable portion, but it's never too early to find out how matters stand. I'm guessing ten thousand?"

"Then you would be surprised."

The baron's eyes lighted. "*More?*"

Simon tired of the game. "A word to the wise, Draycott. Celia might be willing to accept a baron, considering her grandfather's rank, but our great-uncle has much higher plans than that for her. He told me just last night that he expects her to snare an earl at least."

Draycott snorted. "That'll be worth seeing."

Simon shrugged, doing his best to look mysterious. He wasn't stretching the truth, for Uncle Rupert had uttered exactly those words over their port – and even though Simon was pretty certain Uncle Rupert had been exercising his bent for sarcasm when he said it, what the baron didn't know wouldn't hurt him. This popinjay, basing his interest in Celia purely on the amount of her dowry, deserved to be smacked down.

Lord Stone lingered over his port and appeared in no hurry to rejoin the ladies. Baron Draycott eventually said, "Stone, old top, shouldn't we make a move toward the drawing room before the ladies get tired of waiting for us and toddle off to their beds?"

Lord Stone cast a look at the carved-plaster ceiling with a long-suffering sigh. "The harpies will be lying in wait no matter when we arrive." He drained his glass. "Gentlemen?"

Simon had mixed feelings about leaving the safety of the dining room to join a covey of ladies who were on the hunt for husbands. Regardless of the way he'd tweaked Celia, he had no intention of finding himself leg-shackled by the end of the week.

But he told himself it was foolish to hesitate, for he was perfectly safe from the ladies' wiles. A mere Mr. Montrose was hardly a plump-enough rabbit to interest the Carew sisters so long as higher-ranking gentlemen remained in the lists, so he could safely amuse himself by watching the competition, or perhaps even by dabbling in the sport of flirtation. It might be entertaining to see if he could throw a few barriers in Draycott's path as the baron devoted himself to one or more of his three potential brides.

Simon debated whether he should warn Celia about the baron. Draycott's tedious pomposity would surely be evident to her soon enough. But what if Celia thought the baron's awkwardness was only a quirk, brought about by his self-conscious eagerness to impress her?

She was such an innocent – her mother had raised her on fairy tales – that it wouldn't be out of reason for the girl to assume that the very first gentleman who showed the barest interest in her must turn out to be her Prince Charming. And since even a man as self-absorbed as Draycott would be smarter than to come straight out with his shallow reasons for courting her, she might be enough of a foggy romantic to accept him regardless of his oddities.

Simon supposed he'd better tell her that she was no more than a number on a list to the baron. Even though he didn't cherish any of the warmer feelings for his cousin, it wasn't as though Simon didn't care what happened to her.

Or for that matter, what happened to his five hundred guineas.

*****

The Carew sisters pounded out a duet on the pianoforte – someone who cherished a more charitable feeling toward the pair than Celia did might have called their effort music – while Lady Hester and Lady Stone exchanged banalities by the fire. They were discussing the gentlemen, and Celia's ears perked when she heard Simon's name.

"A shame such a handsome man is not an eligible match," Hester murmured.

"But it's so much fun to sample the merchandise, no? Now *and* later." Lady Stone gave a wicked little chuckle as Hester turned slightly pink.

Celia's jaw went slack. Surely their hostess wasn't seriously suggesting to an unmarried girl that she plan ahead for a lover – but it seemed to Celia there was no other interpretation. Hester had obviously understood, too. Unless that becoming flush meant she wasn't just looking ahead to a day when a complaisant husband wouldn't mind her taking a lover, but that she'd already – as Lady Stone put it – *sampled the merchandise*. The notion that Simon might be carrying on some kind of *affaire*, right under Uncle Rupert's nose, was a facer.

Lady Stone's companion returned from her errand, and Celia discreetly patted the chair beside her own, inviting Jane to sit.

Jane paused to murmur something to her employer and then crossed the room. "Is it only me," she said quietly, tipping her head toward the pianoforte, "or would you rather listen to cats yowling?"

Celia choked on a giggle.

Jane turned red, as if startled by her own words. "Your pardon, Miss Overton."

"Do please call me Celia. And I lost my composure because I was thinking much the same thing. Shameful of me, I know, but…"

Jane smiled, and suddenly the sparkle in her wide-set brown eyes lent grace and charm to what had seemed an ordinary countenance. "Still, I should not have said it. After just a few weeks in Lady Stone's employ, I fear I have forgotten how to hold my peace."

Celia must have looked as puzzled as she felt. Wasn't saying only what the employer wished to hear the very definition of a successful companion? Of course, Lady Stone *was* something of an original… but even the most sharp-tongued lady seldom appreciated when someone in her employ was equally outspoken.

"Lady Stone likes you very much, by the way," Jane went on. "How did you happen to meet her?"

"My uncle was taking the waters in Tunbridge Wells last summer, when…"

Dimity, her piano piece finally finished, sank into the chair next to Jane. "Prudence insists that practice is never wasted, but I refuse to play more until the gentlemen arrive. I assume you did not have the benefit of lessons or a pianoforte, Miss Overton?"

"I don't know why you'd think that," Celia said calmly. "But it is true that the pianoforte has never been my favorite pastime."

In the silence, Lady Stone's raspy voice carried further than usual. "Your father insists on a title for you, Hester? But you'd still be *my lady*, you know, no matter who you married."

Dimity sniffed. "As though Lady Hester needs instruction from Lady Stone in proper forms of address!"

Prudence came to join her sister. "She's perfectly correct, but it would be just too uncomfortable, I'd think, for a couple to be addressed as Lady Hester and – for example – the mere Mr. Montrose."

"*I* wouldn't be interested in a man with no title," Dimity went on, "though I could wish that Lord Stone was a livelier sort of man."

"And less well-named," Jane said under her breath. "He's immovable as a boulder."

Celia bit her lip to keep from laughing. From the little she'd observed of him, she supposed Lord Stone did bear a certain resemblance to a rock.

Prudence surveyed her sister. "Have you set your mind on him then, Dimity?"

Dimity shrugged. "Well, not so firmly that I couldn't be persuaded otherwise. But since he and Lord Lockwood are the only earls present, I shall defer to you as the older sister and leave Lord Lockwood for you… Oh, here are the gentlemen." She smiled brightly as they trooped in.

Celia realized her attempt at sprightly conversation over dinner hadn't won Lord Lockwood's heart, for though he nodded at her across the room, he didn't seek her out.

For an instant, she was almost hurt. But how foolish it was, when she had found his company tedious, to feel wounded because he didn't immediately pursue the acquaintance! Besides, she noted, he didn't seek out the other young ladies either; he took a seat beside Lady Stone, opposite Lady Hester. Celia shot a sideways look at Prudence, who appeared not to have noticed either her sister's gibe or Lockwood's avoidance.

Baron Draycott made a beeline for the Carew sisters. "You promised to play for us," he reminded Prudence. "I shall turn the pages if you like."

Viscount Billings was only a few steps behind him, and as the sisters returned to the pianoforte, he followed without casting even a glance at Celia or Jane.

"We seem to be invisible," Celia said, with an effort to be cheerful.

"Invisibility is a companion's lot," Jane answered. "Perhaps sitting by me makes you hard to see as well."

Celia scarcely heard her, for the last pair of gentlemen to come into the room – Lord Stone and

Simon – stopped near the door and appeared to be completely absorbed in their conversation. Celia wondered what they'd found in common. Perhaps Simon had taken their hostess's advice to heart and was already attempting to convince Lord Stone to invest in one of Uncle Rupert's schemes.

She turned back to Jane, noting that the young woman's gaze had also fallen on the newcomers.

"What's the story about your cousin?" Jane asked.

The question sounded almost careless, but Celia wasn't fooled; there could be nothing casual about Jane's interest.

Clearly Jane was a born lady, but if she'd had a wealthy family she wouldn't be working as a companion to a crotchety old female. Without a decent dowry or an elevated rank of her own, Jane was hardly the sort of bride a titled gentleman would seek out. Only if one of them tumbled madly into love with her would he even consider making an offer.

Therefore it was no wonder that Jane's eye had fallen on Simon. A pleasant young man of reasonable good looks, possessing excellent manners but not acting high in the instep, must seem very inviting to a young woman in Jane's circumstances. Because his money came from trade, Simon was just as much on the outskirts of society as Jane was. For Jane, the fact that he earned a living with his own efforts – the very thing that made the Carew sisters turn up their noses at him – might even seem an attractive characteristic.

The entire idea sat oddly on Celia's mind, possibly because Jane's circumstances were an uncomfortable reminder of her own. If Uncle Rupert were to remain adamant about his refusal to fund a dowry for her, then Celia too would have to captivate a gentleman so completely that what she brought to the marriage wouldn't matter to him – and that fact was much less fun to think about than Simon's possible entanglements.

Jane cleared her throat. "Miss Overton?"

Oh. Yes. Jane asked about Simon. A friend would warn her, Celia supposed – and though they had met only hours before, she counted the young woman as a friend. "My cousin has been quite taken with Lady Hester."

Jane sounded skeptical. "I would never have guessed it. They've scarcely looked at each other."

So she'd been watching him, had she? "Simon is too discreet to wear his heart on his sleeve. As for Lady Hester, she can flirt with him any time at home, but to do so here might risk upsetting the opportunity for a match her parents would approve."

Jane frowned.

Ruthlessly, Celia changed the subject. "You've been just a few weeks with Lady Stone, you said?"

"About two months. Her companions appear not to last long, for I believe I am the third this year."

"She must be very difficult to work for."

"Oh, it's not that, really. I mean, it *is* a lot of work – arranging this house party, for instance – but she's not unpleasant or even demanding."

"Why is she giving this party, anyway? I appreciate that she's adopting the role of fairy godmother, but I'd think the wedding alone would be enough, without adding complications."

"Well, the Carew sisters and Lady Hester are to be Imogene's bridesmaids, so they'd be here nonetheless. But to be perfectly honest, I think Lady Stone sweeps in and takes over simply to annoy her nephew. Rockhill is his – but as long as he remains unmarried, she's the ranking lady, and she doesn't hesitate to exercise what she sees as her rights."

"So the poor man might end up married to Dimity Carew just to avoid having Lady Stone take over his house whenever she feels inclined?"

"Well, there's a dilemma for you," Jane said dryly. "I wonder if he'd rather share his home with Lady Stone for a fortnight now and then, or with Dimity Carew every day."

Celia couldn't stop the laugh which bubbled forth and filled the sudden silence which had fallen across the drawing room as the last few notes of Miss Carew's pianoforte piece ended. Everyone looked at Celia, and she felt her face sizzle with embarrassment. "I beg your pardon, Miss Carew," she said awkwardly. "I was not amused by your performance."

Dimity gasped.

Now I've made things even worse. "I meant, of course, that it was not the performance which I found amusing. Your musical abilities are quite…"

Dimity glared.

Was there any way to save the situation? In desperation, Celia began to applaud, and slowly the others joined in.

Baron Draycott let go of the last sheet of music and leaned over the pianoforte to murmur something to Dimity. But he wasn't looking at her; he caught Celia's eye instead, grinned, and winked.

She gulped and gave him a tiny smile in return. It appeared Baron Draycott had a sense of humor – so perhaps she'd found a kindred spirit after all.

But as she settled back in her chair, feeling more hopeful than she had all evening, she caught Simon looking at her, his brow creased in a frown.

Friday

Fortunately, Simon enjoyed quiet, because Rockhill's breakfast room offered plenty of it. It also provided food in quantities that would feed an army, along with enough servants – all silently bowing and scraping – to give a man a serious case of nerves. Finally he succeeded in shooing them away.

Perhaps it was just as well he himself was required to work for a living, for it was certain he'd be no success at the layabout lifestyle the gentlemen of this party seemed to enjoy.

He was polishing off a sizeable breakfast when Lady Stone's colorless little companion – Joan? Jean? – came in. She paused in the doorway, obviously startled.

Simon rose. "Good morning, Miss… I was beginning to think no one in the house bothered with breakfast at all."

"I'm sure the gentlemen will be down before long, with the promise of a day's hunting to lure them from their beds." She colored, as though the reference had been a naughty one.

If such a mild entendre embarrassed her, how did she manage to cope with their hostess? Lady Stone appeared to exercise no reins at all on her tongue.

"The best part of the day will be gone by then," he observed, "and the game will probably have gone to shelter – though I presume the birds won't mind more sportsmanlike odds. May I help you to a slice of ham? I suggested to the butler that it wasn't necessary to have three footmen watching every bite I took, but now the entire staff seems to have found occupation elsewhere."

A rustle from the doorway drew his attention as Celia came in, fresh and dainty in green-sprigged muslin with matching ribbons threaded through the locks of chestnut hair piled atop her head. She glanced around the room and seemed downcast to find only Simon and the companion. "Where is everyone?"

She's looking for Baron Draycott, no doubt.

Simon had made up his mind not to speak to her about the baron. The man was a blowhard, and his questions about Celia's dowry had been both nosy and unsettling, but it had been only talk. He'd paid far more attention last night to the Carew sisters.

But then he and Celia had shared that secret smile across the drawing room…

Simon pushed his plate aside. "If I might have a private conversation with you, cousin? In the hall, perhaps?"

"But I want my breakfast."

"My business will take only a moment."

The companion looked from one to the other and murmured, "I must check on the menus for today, if you will excuse me."

She'd barely cleared the doorway before Celia sat down next to Simon and reached for the teapot. She smelled of something light and summery this morning – rose water, he thought. The scent mixed pleasantly with the steamy aroma rising off her cup.

"That was not well done of you, Simon – sending Jane off without so much as a mouthful to eat. What was so important that you must drive her away?"

"*Jane* – now I remember her name. A warning for you, Celia. Watch out for Draycott."

Celia's eyebrows rose. "What in heaven's name are you talking about? The baron and I have barely exchanged words."

And smiles. But you probably don't realize I noticed that. "He told me last night you're the perfect choice to be a baroness, since you're not the sort to get above yourself."

"How would he know that about me?"

Simon let his voice go dry. "How he came by that notion is an interesting question indeed."

The way she caught her lower lip between her teeth boded no good, he knew from experience.

"The baron is quite an insightful man, it appears." To his annoyance, she sounded intrigued rather than put off. "Perhaps I should try to get to know him better."

Did she really take his insights so lightly? "He's also been totting up how much your dowry must run to, in case he opts to offer for you."

"Well, that makes things easy for you, doesn't it? You need only drop a hint that my expectations are limited to the five hundred guineas I might win from you, and that would put an end to his interest."

"Do you think I'm so unsporting as that?"

"I am comforted that you do not plan to interfere. But of course your freedom is worth five hundred guineas, especially since Uncle Rupert would blame me, not you, for setting his plans awry."

"It appears you're just as insightful as the baron is," Simon muttered.

"Thank you, dear cousin." She leaned closer. The rose-water scent tickled his nose and tugged at something deep inside him, and warning bells went off in Simon's head. "As long as you and I are sharing advice, I couldn't help but notice you've barely spoken a word to Lady Hester."

He knew he should ignore her. Not that it would do any good to try, for when Celia decided to speak her mind, nothing would stop her.

"Pretending not to notice her isn't a bad idea," she went on. "Ignoring her might even help to pique her interest – so long as you don't overdo the thing. But you might do well to pay particular attention to the other young ladies as well. I suspect Hester thinks she has you safely fascinated, always there just off to the side, waiting for the moment when she wants you again."

"Your logic is always fascinating, Celia. Who would you suggest I pay particular attention to?"

"The Carew sisters," she said promptly.

"*Both* of them? I hardly think–"

"It's not as if you're seriously pursuing them – though perhaps you should, for they are very plump in the pockets, I understand. Their dowries will be so large even you couldn't turn up your nose. However, the point is if you were to win interest from a Carew sister, Hester would have to take notice."

"I shall bear that in mind."

Celia smiled suddenly, a naughty elfin grin that lit up her eyes and made her face glow. "There's no reason you can't do it, Simon. You can be charming – when you try."

No wonder the baron was intrigued. When she smiled like that, every man in the vicinity must feel heat sparkling across his skin.

"A compliment from my cousin," he said wryly. "I shall mark this day down as notable."

Celia sat up straight, tilting her head with an ear toward the door. "I think... yes, I am persuaded I hear Baron Draycott in the entrance hall. You will excuse me, Simon?"

Without waiting for him to answer, much less rise respectfully from his chair, she was gone.

Simon shook his head and decided to have another cup of coffee rather than wander out into the hall to watch Celia make a fool of herself. He had done all he could; she had been warned.

It wouldn't be his fault if she took the caution as a challenge instead.

*****

Celia had been right that she'd heard Baron Draycott's drawl, but she didn't realize until she was almost at the foot of the grand staircase that he was descending with a Carew sister on each arm. She glanced over her shoulder, thankful to see that Simon hadn't followed her. Amusing as the situation would no doubt have been for him, Celia wasn't certain she could restrain herself from giving him a swift kick in the shins if he dared to laugh at her.

The baron and his two damsels reached the main floor and he bowed elegantly to each of the sisters as he excused himself. "Though of course I am loathe to leave you, Lord Stone wants to get an early start in order to bag enough birds for a feast tonight in the bride's honor."

Dimity pouted prettily – at least the young woman must have thought her pout made her look charming, or she wouldn't have let her mouth twist like that. Prudence sighed as the baron went off toward the back of the house where the gun room must be located.

"I do think the baron is quite the best-looking man here," Dimity said.

"At least, the best-looking *eligible* man," Prudence added.

Celia rolled her eyes. The baron wasn't unpleasant in looks, though he'd be greatly improved if he allowed his valet to tame the too-long, too-curly hair that made him look like he was wearing a small yellow lamb on his head. She wouldn't be at all surprised if he ended up tangled in a thicket while seeking pheasants or quail.

But of course hair – unlike so many other qualities a gentleman might possess – would be an easy thing to fix; all a wife would need to do was gently suggest the change.

As for the rest – Draycott was tall enough to be impressive, only a couple of inches shorter than Simon. His shoulders were wide, though she wondered if his tailor had to add padding; there had been a suspicious softness about his pale blue coat last night.

"Miss Overton," Dimity said. "I didn't see you there in the shadows. What a surprise that you're down already. I thought perhaps you would enjoy the rare opportunity to lie abed."

"I enjoy rising early, especially when I can ride."

"Really?" Prudence said. "We must make certain you have the opportunity to do so, then."

Doubt dripped from her voice and burned Celia's skin as if it had been acid. *She sounds as if she expects me to fall off my horse.*

"Not this morning, however," Dimity added hastily. "There's little point in riding if the gentlemen don't come along. Lady Stone suggested that since the hunters will be gone much of the day, we might entertain ourselves with a walk to the village."

A walk, no matter the destination, was preferable to being shut up inside all day with the Misses Carew. Celia scolded herself for allowing the rude thought to cross her mind.

Just as Celia opened her mouth to agree, Prudence added, "You'll come, of course? I'm sure you can give us advice about any bargains to be found in the village shops. Cloth and that sort of thing."

Celia's tongue seemed to stick to the roof of her mouth. *Does she think I run a loom for my uncle?*

"I have the greatest difficulty, myself, in telling one fabric from another," Prudence went on, "so I generally end up buying the most expensive."

From the foot of the stairs, Jane said mildly, "I hardly think Miss Overton is personally acquainted with a cloth factory."

She had descended so quietly Celia hadn't realized she was there. Apparently the Carew sisters hadn't either, for Dimity snapped, "I do wish you'd stop sneaking around, Jane!"

"Your pardon. Lady Hester prefers to remain abed this morning, and Lady Imogene has the final fitting for her wedding garb. But if everyone else is ready for our walk…"

Eventually they were, though Celia wondered if the sisters were dawdling in the hope the hunting party might give up their day out and return to the house. When they finally set out across Rockhill's wide lawns, Celia fell into step with Jane, while the Carew sisters walked a few yards behind, once more discussing the gentlemen of the party.

"I do hope it's not Lord Lockwood who offers for me," Dimity said as they turned onto a well-worn footpath. "Just imagine sharing the marriage bed with someone who is so very old."

"What about Lord Billings?" Celia asked. "He's quite young."

Prudence cast a pitying look in her direction. "They call him Lord Bilious, you know."

Jane nodded. "It's true he has a very delicate stomach. The cook has been distraught over his requirements for special foods."

"According to the *ton*," Prudence said, "he may not live long enough to survive his father. His wife would be left with nothing. No real title, for it would go to the next heir, and no money either."

"Such a shame that Lord Billings is unwell," Jane murmured. "Of course, Mr. Montrose is quite good-looking."

Dimity sighed. "Such a pity he isn't eligible. But no matter how large the weaver's fortune, it just won't do."

"You astound me," Celia said.

"Oh, it's different for you, of course, Miss Overton, because the fact that your money comes from trade can be disguised somewhat by your husband's standing – assuming that some gentleman should offer for you. But for a man to bring the whiff of trade into a marriage..." Dimity shook her head sadly.

So much for Celia's half-formed plan to keep Simon too busy with his own flirtations to interfere with her efforts. It had seemed such a good idea at breakfast. But if the Carew sisters weren't likely to take him seriously...

Then perhaps you should give them a reason.

Celia spoke before she could talk herself out of the notion. "It seems foolish to assess a gentleman based only on his current standing, not taking into account his potential as you did with Lord Billings."

Prudence looked offended. "Of course it would be short-sighted."

Dimity frowned. "Are you suggesting someone here is in line for a grand inheritance?" Celia could almost see her ticking names off a list. "But all the gentlemen are in full possession of their estates except for Lord Bilious... I mean, Lord Billings."

An imp seemed to take hold of Celia's brain. "Perhaps you didn't realize Mr. Montrose is in line for a title." Her conscience pinged, but she silenced it. She hadn't told an untruth... not exactly. As the great-grandson of a viscount, Simon must be in some line of succession. The fact there were probably twenty male uncles and cousins ahead of him in that line by now was immaterial, really.

Prudence sniffed. "If that were the case, Hester wouldn't be so uninterested."

"Perhaps she doesn't know it," Celia murmured. "It's something he prefers not to speak of. Oh, here's the village. Which shop should we visit first, do you think?"

*****

When Simon reached the drawing room that evening, he was relieved to find that his partner for dinner was to be Lady Stone's companion. At least he wouldn't be subjected to another few hours of scorn from a Carew sister.

So Celia thought he should try courting one or the other of those termagants! Had the minx lost her wits entirely, or had she simply been trying to distract him from her odd fascination with Baron Draycott?

He tried to catch her eye across the room, but she was listening intently to Viscount Billings, who was probably telling her the history of his stomach complaints. Nothing serious could possibly develop there, Simon knew. Though he was not an intimate of Lady Hester's brother, he knew Billings well enough to understand that the man had far too great an opinion of his status to consider a girl in Celia's position. Perhaps more to the point, he was too careful of his various ailments to have time to pay romantic attention to a female.

Prudence Carew strolled across the room directly toward Simon. A brilliant smile curved her lips but did not, he noted, quite reach her eyes. "I was so looking forward to getting to know you better." Her eyelids fluttered at such a rate he thought she must be trying to blink away a painful speck of dust. "In fact, I asked Jane to switch dinner partners with me tonight – but the foolish girl insisted her arrangements could not be upset." Her voice dropped. "If I might offer a word of advice – Mr. Montrose?"

The instant's hesitation made him wonder if she'd forgotten his name. "I shall always be eager to receive a lady's wisdom." *If she possesses any.*

She languidly waved her fan, inviting him to lean closer. "A gentleman cannot be too careful where a female of such questionable background is concerned. A companion, after all… I bring it up only to warn you that Jane's too-friendly ways may hide an ulterior motive. I think, myself, that she has fixed her eye on you."

Simon, finding himself speechless, settled for bowing politely.

"But perhaps it is for the best that she refused to be accommodating this evening," Prudence murmured. "Tomorrow is the ball Lady Stone is hosting for the bridal couple. You will be not only my dinner companion, but you can lead me out in the first dance." She smiled as though she had presented him with an award and joined Lord Stone just as the dinner gong sounded.

Simon intercepted a bright-eyed look from Celia as she strolled past with her hand on Viscount Billings' arm. She looked curiously happy – but surely she couldn't be finding anything in Lord Bilious's conversation to so thoroughly fascinate her.

Beside Simon, Baron Draycott released a long breath. "Miss Overton is incandescent tonight. Just look at how that glorious hair of hers reflects the light. I can't help but think how it would look spread out across a pillow in the glow of a branch of candles."

Simon turned to stare at him. "Perhaps my hearing is at fault, my lord? Because if you really said you're lusting after my cousin and imagining taking her to your bed, I would find it necessary to defend the lady's honor."

Draycott tipped his head back and studied Simon down the length of his aquiline nose.

He's considering whether I can handle myself in a duel.

The baron opted not to test the point. "No, no – not at all. You must have heard me wrong, Montrose. If you'll excuse me … Miss Dimity. There you are. We are to be partners tonight, I understand." He reached for her arm.

She stood firm. "I fear, Mr. Montrose, that I may have been a trifle rude last night at dinner. I was not feeling well then, and I do hope you will accept my apologies." She dropped a tiny curtsy and let the baron draw her away.

Simon blinked in astonishment. *Both* Carew sisters had experienced a change of heart?

Jane strolled up, cleared her throat, and smiled. Simon, belatedly realizing they were the last in the drawing room, offered his arm. He only hoped she wasn't going to lean on him too heavily, for he was feeling off-balance – as if the Axminster carpet in the drawing room had suddenly turned to quicksand under his toes.

What have you done, Silly Overton? And why?

Because if there was one thing he was certain of, it was that the curious change in the atmosphere was somehow Celia's doing.

Saturday

Celia had managed to remain on the far side of the room from Simon all evening, though only by devoting herself to young Lord Bilious – *Oh, dear, now I'm doing it too* – and the endless recital of his digestive problems, to the point that simply holding down her own dinner seemed a notable accomplishment.

Perhaps it was only her imagination – or her guilty conscience – which suggested that every now and then Simon cast a smoldering glare across the room at her, because whenever she dared to steal a peek in his direction, he seemed to be enjoying the company. Prudence and Dimity had nudged Jane aside after dinner, though they seemed careful to divide their attention equally between Simon, Lord Stone, and Baron Draycott. Lady Hester, sharing a settee with Lord Lockwood, couldn't seem to keep her gaze from straying to the group by the fireplace, where she'd clearly rather be. The bride and groom had eyes only for each other.

Really, it was as good as a play to watch them all. Celia hesitated when the evening came to an end and it was time to go up to bed, because she found herself thinking how much fun it would be to stay and tweak Simon a bit. Sanity prevailed, however, and she meekly followed Lady Hester and the Carew sisters up the stairs.

But on Saturday morning when she came down to join the others who were riding out to view the countryside around Rockhill, Simon was standing in her path at the foot of the stairs. She faltered for a moment, then gave him a bright smile and walked around him to join the others milling aimlessly in the entrance hall.

Hester came down a few minutes later wearing a dark green habit, and their hostess followed.

Lady Stone paused on the stairs and looked out over the group. "I suppose some society matrons would find me ridiculously lax in allowing my party of young people to go off on a jaunt without me to chaperone. But I no longer ride, and it would be poor sport for you to be limited to the roads my chaise could take." Lord Billings opened his mouth as if to argue, but Lady Stone went straight on. "In any event it seems to me that the ladies will all be quite adequately chaperoned. Lady Hester has her brother to look after her; Dimity and Prudence have each other; and I'm relying on you, Mr. Montrose, to keep your cousin safe."

Celia coughed, swallowed at the same moment, and choked. "What about Jane?" she managed finally. "I'm certain she and I could act as each other's duennas."

"Jane will be overseeing everyone," Lady Stone said crisply. "Along with Imogene, of course, if she can take her gaze off her betrothed."

"Eh?" the bride said vaguely. "Did you speak, Aunt Lucinda?"

Lady Stone sighed. "No, dear. Enjoy yourselves, children – but not so much that I have to explain subsequent events to your parents."

Chattering, the Carew sisters headed straight out the massive main door. On the gravel sweep in front of the house, a half-dozen grooms waited with horses already saddled.

Celia ran her gaze across the mounts, seeing a wide range of animals, from a neat little bay mare who seemed to dance in place under her sidesaddle to a big and placid gelding who was more interested in eating a potted plant than in prospective riders.

Dimity pointed at the bay mare. "That's the one I want."

The groom holding the mare shook his head. "Sorry, miss, but this one's intended for Miss Overton – right, Mr. Montrose?"

Simon nodded. "Celia?"

She noticed a shilling pass smoothly from his hand to the groom's, and then Simon helped her up into the saddle and took the reins of a rangy roan gelding for himself. Celia nudged the mare to the edge of the gravel to wait for the others to mount; Simon sidestepped the gelding over beside her.

She said tartly, "You can chaperone me from further than two feet away."

"This is the appreciation I get for nabbing the best mare in the stable for you?" His voice was a low rumble. "You could have been stuck with that nag Billings is riding."

She looked over the mounts again. "Lord Stone's stable seems a bit thin – so thank you, Simon. But I can hardly further my goals by riding next to you when I might be charming one of the gentlemen. I hope you won't feel it necessary to stick so very close. Or have you changed your mind about wanting me to win my bet? Are you trying to clip my wings?"

"If you prefer the company of the others, go ahead and run away from me."

"I know better than to try," she admitted. "You're too good a horseman."

"From sarcasm to flattery in mere moments. One might wonder why. Perhaps you're feeling – let me guess – guilty?"

She bit her tongue, annoyed that he had read her so well, and tried for an airy tone. "Guilty over what? Not being properly gracious in expressing my gratitude?"

"Because you have some reason to feel guilty."

"What are you yammering about, Simon?"

"Only yesterday you suggested I court the Carew sisters, but before the day was out they seemed to be courting me instead. I cannot help but ask why."

"How modest you are!" Her voice sounded high and tinny. She cleared her throat and tried again. "Perhaps they listened to Jane – who thinks you're quite handsome. Or they may have simply reconsidered their manners and decided to act like ladies."

Simon's eyes narrowed. "Whatever you did, Celia, it's time to undo it."

The line of horses moved down the long carriageway and under the oak trees. Lord Billings, riding the placid gelding, drew up beside her. "Would you care to ride beside me and chat, Miss Overton? I don't believe in rushing around; I find galloping upsets my digestion."

No wonder he'd started to argue that Lady Stone – and her chaise – should accompany them. Celia didn't dare meet Simon's gaze for fear of bursting into giggles.

But Simon didn't try to catch her eye. He shifted his weight in the saddle and touched his heel to the roan's flank, breaking into a canter which left Celia stuck with Lord Billings and feeling entirely bereft.

How utterly foolish, when she'd asked him to leave her alone!

But of course it wasn't Simon abandoning her which made her feel so out of sorts. Her body ached with regret; she was so far in the wrong she could barely see daylight. What had possessed her to tell such a taradiddle, anyway? – much less convince herself that Simon wouldn't notice? Of course he would catch her out; he had never been slow about adding together random bits and pieces and coming up with a full – and usually quite accurate – assessment.

But what was she supposed to do about it when she was stuck at the back of the line with Lord Billings, of all people?

*****

The day was beautiful and bright, and their destination was a tumbledown abbey which stood atop a hill, overlooking a long green valley. The site had been so long abandoned that trees had grown up everywhere. Lush vines shrouded heaps of fallen stone and piles of dark red Tudor brick, making it difficult to tell where one ruined building ended and the next began. Enough of the carved stone cloister pillars remained, however, to define a space just right for strolling. An almost painfully-clear blue sky arched overhead.

A perfect day, in Celia's estimation. At least it would have been if not for her own folly.

The two grooms who had accompanied the party helped the ladies to dismount near the cloister, taking the horses off to a makeshift paddock at the far side of the abbey, but the gentlemen rode on with them. Jane was apparently counting noses to be certain no one had disappeared, and Hester and Prudence wandered past a heap of stone and brick to where the view of the valley was unobstructed. Imogene and her betrothed had dawdled far behind even Lord Billings' slow pace.

For a moment Celia found herself alone with Dimity. She knew she must seize the opportunity, for there might not be another chance when the gentlemen were not present to absorb attention.

But what to say?

So sorry about the bouncer I told yesterday, but Simon has the same chance of inheriting a title as Lord Stone's cook does.

"It's just as well you were stuck with that mare," Dimity said. "She's good-looking, but even with an excellent rider, she couldn't have kept up with Lord Stone. I wonder why he keeps her."

Even with a good rider? If politeness hadn't kept her jogging alongside Lord Billings, Celia and the mare would have been far in front, enjoying a wild run. The insult made her bones itch, but diplomacy was called for if she was to fix the mess she'd made yesterday.

Dimity glanced around as if to make certain they couldn't be overheard. "It's the oddest thing, but you were right. Hester *doesn't* seem to know about Mr. Montrose." She dropped her voice further. "His coming into a title, I mean."

"You told her?" But what had Celia expected? It was far too good a tale not to share.

Dimity drew herself up and tossed her head. "Of course not. You said he prefers the matter not be discussed, so I did no more than hint – only to find out how much Hester knew, you see."

"I beg you will forget I said anything at all. I should not have brought the matter up."

"I only wish you hadn't spoken in front of Jane and given her ideas. But you can count on Prudence and me not to let anything slip. My sister and I are excellent at keeping secrets." Dimity's eyes gleamed. "Particularly from Hester – and especially when it's something she would very much enjoy knowing."

Especially when they think it gives them an advantage in the marriage market. If I can't convince her I was exaggerating, they're still going to be after Simon, and he'll be even more annoyed with me.

"I – Well…" Celia plunged in. "The truth of the matter is it's a far more distant relationship than I implied yesterday."

"You mean he's *not* in line to inherit a title?"

"Not directly. I mean, I don't really know how the thing stands, but…" Dimity's eyes brightened, and Celia realized that kind of mealy-mouthed explanation wouldn't do at all; she must extinguish all hope if the Carew sisters were to go back to treating Simon normally. "I'm certain the possibility is vanishingly small. Of course you can understand how embarrassing it would be for everyone if it were to be mentioned. I just hope my misstatement doesn't lead to confusion about my cousin's circumstances."

"You mean you lied, and he's not an eligible suitor after all."

The flat statement struck Celia like a blow across the face. Not the part about her fabrication, for on the entire long ride she'd been regretting the crack in her character which had allowed her to go so far astray. But for Dimity to dismiss Simon coldly because a title was the only thing that mattered to her…

Perhaps it's just as well she thinks as she does. Simon deserved something far better than these title-hunting vixens, that much was certain.

"Mr. Montrose has many merits and good qualities," Celia said stiffly, "even though a title is not one of them."

She hadn't seen Jane come up to them until the companion gave a polite little cough. "Shall we walk over to take in the view?"

Dimity strutted off to join her sister.

"I beg your pardon, but I couldn't help overhearing," Jane said. "That can't have been an easy conversation."

"I hope my overstatement will go no further. I was very wrong to say anything at all."

Jane smiled. "Of course, my dear."

Celia relaxed. *What a lovely young woman she is.* She wondered if Simon had noticed; he'd seen through the Carew sisters quickly enough. Jane would make an excellent wife for him, if he could just look past Lady Hester.

It would be a shame if Simon had indeed set his heart on Hester. Sadness rippled through her at the thought.

But it would be even worse if he were to marry Jane while Celia went home without an offer. Then she'd not only owe him five hundred guineas, but she'd never hear the end of it.

*****

The ball Lady Stone had arranged in honor of the upcoming marriage was really too thin of company to be worthy of the name, with only a dozen couples taking the floor for the first country dance. Prudence complained about the small size of the orchestra, and Dimity fussed over the lack of dance cards.

Baron Draycott requested the pleasure of leading Celia out in the evening's first country dance. His conversation at dinner – the first time they'd really talked – had been too shallow to let her assess the man, but at least he wanted to get to know her better. Not that dancing made things any easier; the steps of the country dance kept them apart more than together.

She looked down the row of dancers and saw that Simon was opposite Prudence, whose smile seemed to glow as she offered him her hands. Uneasiness swept through Celia and she missed her own cue.

The baron looked annoyed for an instant before he smiled and said, "It must be difficult to keep track of the dance when you're not used to the figures."

Celia, annoyed at once more being written off as a rube, forced her attention back to her own steps, circling and dipping with him, changing partners, swinging through the figures with only one other misstep – when she and Simon were partnered briefly.

"I thought I told you to fix it," he said, but before she could answer the music swept him away once more.

The country dance was followed by a waltz, and from the corner of her eye, Celia saw Simon coming toward her. She studiously ignored him to smile invitingly at Lord Lockwood – but the earl led Dimity out instead.

Simon's bow was polite, but his tone wasn't. "It looks as though I'm your only option, Silly."

"I'd rather sit this one out."

"No, you wouldn't. You love to waltz – even with me."

That was true, and she tapped her toe as the music started. "All right, but only because looking like a wallflower would be worse."

Simon was an excellent dancer, she admitted as he swirled her around the room. He should have had no shortage of partners, which meant he had sought her out for another reason.

I told you to fix it…

He smiled down at her, a challenging glint in his eyes, but before he could speak, Celia said, "It's not my fault Prudence still seems enamored of you. Perhaps she discovered that she likes you after all. I can't understand why she would feel that way, but…"

"Give it some thought," he said cryptically. "How are your suitors ranking at the moment? Is there a favorite?"

"If there was, I wouldn't tell *you*!"

He smiled. "Draycott didn't win your heart over dinner?"

"Pleasant though it is to hear praise of my gleaming hair, my sparkling eyes, and my charming demeanor—"

"Hmm. As a matter of fact, your hair *does* gleam, and your eyes *do* sparkle."

Celia's heartbeat quickened – no doubt because she was unaccustomed to hearing anything flattering from Simon.

"But your demeanor?" His tone was matter of fact, but his dimple flashed, the sure indication he was teasing her. "Charming? He was telling quite a bouncer there."

She glared at him. "As I was saying, I'd have much rather heard about his home, or his horses, or his plans for his estates—"

"That's a bit mercenary of you."

" — or his family. And I don't mean their noble ancestry, but what he thinks of them. Whether he has sisters, or what his mother is like."

"So he's still in the running, then? I was beginning to be concerned about your attachment to Lord Billings. Having you around all the time would take his mind off his digestion – though I'll warrant you wouldn't improve it."

How very like Simon – to be more concerned about Lord Bilious than about his own cousin. Celia would have made a face at him, but he swept her around in a graceful turn and she remembered how many people were watching, so she gave him a brilliant smile instead, and when the dance ended she demonstrated her best curtsy.

He laughed at her and went off to dance with Jane. Lord Stone, in his stiff way, came across the room to partner Celia.

Midway through the evening the orchestra took a break, and the ladies retired upstairs to check their hair. The Carew sisters' bedroom door was open as Celia passed, and she saw Dimity's maid on the floor at her feet, mending a torn ruffle.

"I believe her," Dimity said firmly.

"Which time?" Prudence asked tartly.

"You didn't hear her stumbling through the explanation. I'd swear she was sorry—"

"Sorry she told us, yes. I suspect she thought better of it because she wants him for herself. Did you see the way she smiled at him when they were waltzing?"

Celia knew she should have realized it wouldn't be easy to fix the misunderstanding.

But wanting Simon for herself? The idea was ludicrous. How foolish could two girls be?

Well, it is the Carews. Perhaps that explains everything.

*****

Prudence snagged another country dance with Simon, as did Dimity – who must have come around to her sister's way of thinking. Or perhaps she just wanted to preserve all her options. But when the time came for the supper waltz, Simon presented himself to Celia once more.

She shook her head. "I can't waltz with you twice in an evening."

"You don't want to waltz with anyone else here. Draycott stepped on Miss Dimity's hem. Lord Lockwood moves like an elephant. Lord Tavish can't see beyond his bride, and Lord Stone…"

"Go away!"

"I am heartbroken," he said, but he went – and all through Celia's waltz with Lord Bilious – *Billings*! – she regretted her choice. The viscount rattled the entire time about the shortcomings of Lord Stone's kitchen, which at least left her free to think.

What was Simon up to? Was he *trying* to make the Carew sisters believe he was courting his cousin? Surely not – but he might be applying the advice Celia herself had given him, only in a different direction. She'd advised him to court the Carews so Lady Hester couldn't take him for granted. But with the two sisters taking him far too seriously for comfort, had he decided to focus on Celia instead?

What a buffle-headed, dicked-in-the-nob thing for him to do!

*****

When the ball finally ended, Celia dawdled till she was almost the last to go upstairs, but she had no opportunity to catch Simon alone. Tomorrow, perhaps? – but they'd be going to church, and Lady Stone had mentioned a picnic. Something had to be done now.

Her maid was waiting in her bedroom, half-asleep by the fire, but Celia dismissed her. "I'll get myself to bed, Daisy."

She waited anxiously, her bedroom door barely cracked open, until the house had quieted. Then Celia crept down the darkened corridor toward the room where Jane had directed Simon on the day they arrived. Her heart thundered at the audacity of what she was doing – sneaking into a man's room, without even carrying a candle to make it seem she was on some legitimate errand, if someone were to spot her.

But as she neared the corner where the two corridors intersected, Simon's door creaked open. Instinct saved her, making her duck into a shadowed niche at the top of the stairs. She peeked out in time to see Lady Hester slipping into Simon's room.

Celia's heart almost stopped. Not only was Hester visiting a man in his bedroom, but the pale pink ball gown she'd worn that evening had given way to a plain dark wrapper which, along with her black hair, made her almost disappear in the unlit corridor.

Celia waited for as long as she dared, but Simon's door remained firmly closed. Finally, still reeling from the shock, she tiptoed back to her room.

So that was the real secret, was it? Simon and Lady Hester were playing at indifference in public – but in the shadows of the night, things were very different indeed.

Sunday

The site for their picnic was a small lake which lay behind Rockhill House, on the far side of the expanse of gardens – and Lady Stone made it clear, when they gathered on the terrace behind the house, that they were expected to walk there. Celia didn't mind; the faint breeze which caressed her face and teased at the pink ribbons on her wide-brimmed hat carried the scent of heliotrope, and in the elm trees which bordered the garden, birds warbled.

"The stroll will do you all good," Lady Stone announced as Lord Billings helped her into the chaise directly below the terrace. "I know I would enjoy the exercise myself, if only I were able."

"She's *able* to do whatever she really wants," Dimity muttered. "And why is Lord Bilious allowed to ride with her if we cannot?"

Celia shrugged. "I'd rather walk than have Lord Stone shoot nasty looks at me over how the chaise wheels are cutting up the lawns."

Dimity looked thoughtfully at the ruts, and a moment later she had crossed the terrace to lay her hand possessively on his lordship's arm while she commiserated about his aunt's carelessness.

Prudence narrowed her eyes as she inspected the company. "Perhaps I'll settle for Lord Lockwood, since Mr. Montrose and Lady Hester seem to be planning to walk together."

Celia whipped around to see for herself. Simon and Lady Hester stood at a corner of the terrace, looking so intent that they might as well have been alone on the moon. Simon shook his head. A moment later, when Lord Lockwood approached the pair, Lady Hester took his arm with only a hint of hesitation, walking away from Simon without a backward glance.

What a very strange little non-conversation that was.

Celia didn't realize she was staring at Simon – trying to read his expression as he watched Hester walk away – until Baron Draycott flourished a bow. "Miss Overton, if I might have the pleasure?"

I'd rather not, she almost said. *I need to make certain Simon is all right.*

But that would only make her seem foolish, so she smiled and laid her hand on his arm. "Of course, sir. Is your home set in such pleasant surroundings as Rockhill?" Perhaps once started on the topic, he would while away the entire walk and let her think in peace.

"That just leaves you and me, Mr. Montrose," Prudence murmured, casting a seemingly-bashful look up at him through her lashes.

Celia noted the unenthusiastic way Simon bowed. "And Miss Jane, of course. Fortunately I have two arms."

Celia bit back a smile, and then sobered. Simon really was gifted at extracting himself from complicated situations. If only he would use that talent to rid himself of Lady Hester before scandal caught up with them!

They walked in a neat little procession, and as they emerged from the trees and the view of the lake opened out before them, Prudence stopped so suddenly that Celia almost ran into her. "*That* is our picnic site?"

Lord Stone sighed, but he didn't answer.

Celia looked past them to where still water reflected a crystal blue sky dotted with lazy clouds. A blue haze lay over the hills beyond. Near the shore, a handful of servants spread cloths across the grass. Baskets stood open; Lord Stone's butler opened wine bottles, and two footmen placed a large upholstered chair where the occupant would have the best view of the lake.

"What's wrong with it?" Celia asked.

Prudence rolled her eyes. "Of course *you* wouldn't know how civilized people picnic. Generally there are tables and real chairs for everyone, not just the hostess because she's old and a bit lame. No wonder Imogene and Lord Tavish are spending the day with his family."

"One expects damask cloths at least," Dimity added, "and china. I wonder if we'll be dining on bread and cheese. What were you thinking, Jane, to call this a picnic?"

"I think it's charming," Celia said.

Simon added, "What is the point of moving outside if one simply takes the entire dining room – and the usual menu – along?"

Jane's grateful smile lit up her face.

She's quite pretty, really – but of course he'll never look at her. Not with Hester slipping into his bedroom.

The footmen passed quietly among them with trays of wineglasses. When everyone had been served, Lord Lockwood raised his glass. "If you'll all lend an ear, I have an announcement. Nuptials are in the air, it seems. This morning, Lady Hester has made me the happiest of men by finally agreeing to my suit." He smiled at his betrothed, who shyly cast her gaze down. "My patience has been rewarded. The arrangements have yet to be finalized, but since the details have been under discussion for some time, our wedding will not be long delayed."

Celia dutifully sipped her wine and tried not to look at Simon. She didn't want to draw attention to him in case his expression let slip how wounded he must feel. But she couldn't keep herself from darting glances his way, and she was pleased to see he was putting a good face on it – drinking the health of the couple and smiling convincingly at Hester. Perhaps that was what Hester had been telling him on the terrace – warning him of the impending announcement.

Dimity muttered, "We should have expected Hester would snag the wealthiest of the gentlemen."

"Why shouldn't she?" Prudence asked reasonably. "You said you didn't want him. And as for me... well, I much prefer someone else." Her gaze, Celia couldn't help but notice, rested warmly on Simon.

*****

Baron Draycott sat beside Celia for their *al fresco* meal, and afterwards he asked if she would care to stroll around the lake with him. When Celia hesitated,

Lady Stone stepped in. "It's such a small lake that the entire shoreline is in view from my chair. You hardly need more chaperoning than that, my dear."

They were barely a quarter of the way around the lake, however, when the baron said, "There's a small folly just off this path, if you would care to see it. I am told it is a jewel of its kind."

"Sir, I hardly think Lady Stone would approve."

He smiled. "With any luck at all, she'll have nodded off for a nap and will never know. But if you insist, we'll stay on the path. I must warn you, however – I'm not getting down on one knee in front of an audience."

"Why would you... oh!"

He turned to face her, seizing both her hands. "My dear Miss Overton, our acquaintance has been short, but my feelings are strong and clear, and Lady Imogene's wedding has made me think of the future. Will you do me the honor of becoming my wife?"

Celia could barely breathe. The baron was everything she had wished for – a gentleman with title and estates, no more than ten years older than she was. He was both presentable and good-natured.

We must hope you find a gentleman who retains his hair and a reasonable number of teeth.

So much for Simon's standards. If anything, the baron had too much hair. And his smile was perfectly pleasant.

But why was she thinking of Simon when she had just received a most flattering offer? Why hadn't she already accepted?

Celia looked past the baron to where sunlight sparkled across ripples on the surface of the lake. What on earth had prompted Simon to take a rowboat – and a young woman – out on the water? No – there were two young women in the boat. Of course; it was Simon, after all.

"Miss Overton?" the baron prompted.

A little voice seemed to whisper in her ear – a voice which sounded uncomfortably like her cousin. *You'd be bored out of your mind with him, you know.*

Celia took a deep breath. "My lord, I do thank you, and I am much flattered by your offer. But I fear we would not be happy together."

"But…" the baron sputtered. "But you were asking about my home! Surely you were hinting that an offer to make you the mistress of that home would not be ill-received."

"I meant only to make conversation, sir. I am sorry if I misled you – but I believe we should not suit. I think it best if we turn back now."

He wheeled around, mouth in a grim line, and set a fast pace back toward the picnic party.

Celia hurried along beside him. What was wrong with her anyway, to turn down an offer that any girl – much less one in her precarious position – should leap at? The fear of boredom was hardly a reason to refuse a marriage proposal!

"So you *are* holding out for a higher title, as your cousin says," the baron muttered. "You'll find yourself disappointed, you know."

Simon had said that? So much for him swearing he wouldn't undercut her efforts! Anger flushed her skin and made her blood pound.

It was a good thing he was out on the lake where she couldn't reach him – or she'd tip him into the water. Or at least give him a good tongue-lashing. At least this way she had time to consider whether yelling at him, or composedly ignoring him, would be the more effective course of action.

Either way, she was finished feeling compassion for Simon. If Hester had broken his heart, he deserved it!

Monday

Celia woke to raindrops plinking against her bedroom windows, and by the time she was dressed the light shower had turned to a steady drizzle. She came into the breakfast room as Simon was mopping up the last of his kidneys and bacon with a bit of bread.

He raised an eyebrow at her riding habit. "You really think we'll be going outside today?"

"You never let rain stop you. Why should I?"

"Admirable, but I can't imagine the Carew sisters going out in this just to see a cathedral, no matter how old or architecturally worthy it might be."

Lightning seared her eyes, bright enough to light the room; a moment later a peal of thunder seemed to rock the house, and rain battered at the windows. "That should decide the matter." Simon pushed his chair back.

Celia tried not to sigh in relief as she went to the sideboard to fill her plate. What if he'd taken up her challenge and the two of them were the only ones interested in a ride?

He didn't leave the room, lingering instead over his tankard of ale. "Let's play billiards. From what I've seen, you're the only decent competition in the house."

Celia was tempted, but she knew better than to give in. "It's one thing to play at home, but no real lady would ever admit to a familiarity with the game. And by the way, no gentleman would sprawl out at the breakfast table as you're doing. What if someone comes in?"

"Perhaps boorish behavior would give the ladies reason to avoid me." He appeared to consider the notion. "Though probably not, with my luck. By the way, I noticed you and the baron didn't finish your walk yesterday."

"How could you see that? You were in a boat with your back to us."

"Not all the time. What happened? Did he make an ungentlemanly remark?"

"He asked me —" Too late, Celia thought better of confiding that she had received and turned down an offer of marriage. The last thing she wanted to do was explain her decision to Simon. "It was too warm for a longer walk."

"It wasn't *that* warm – and I know, since I was rowing across the lake."

"Perhaps it was cooler on the water." Celia abandoned her breakfast. "I'm going up to change. Enjoy your billiards."

"The invitation's still open. Something tells me Lady Stone wouldn't be shocked by your skill."

"I suspect the things that would shock our hostess could be numbered on one hand."

Simon laughed.

At least he didn't seem to be mourning over Hester, Celia thought as she climbed the grand stairway once more.

Giggles from the Carew sisters' bedroom made her want to hurry past, but a voice she hadn't expected drew her to the doorway.

"Come in if you like, Celia," Hester called. "We're discussing what I'm going to do differently when it's time for my wedding. Unlike Imogene, I won't have to depend on my aunt to scratch around for guests."

Celia's spine felt as though Hester had run a flame down it. "Thank you, no. I believe I'll find a quiet corner and a book."

But her book failed to hold her attention, so she mostly sat in the window embrasure of a small sitting room overlooking the garden, watching the flowers beaten down by the rain. The storm was so noisy she almost didn't hear the door open.

Viscount Billings advanced toward her. "Miss Overton, I am pleased to find you by yourself."

Celia made a noncommittal noise and looked down at her book, hoping he'd take the hint and go away.

"And what an out-of-the-way spot you've chosen," he went on. "With the storm blowing so strongly, no one will interrupt."

The tone of his voice made Celia's skin feel tight and over-warm. But it was only Lord Bilious. He probably wanted her to listen to his latest symptoms.

"I have come to offer you my hand in marriage, Miss Overton."

As though he's conveying an enormous honor on me. Of course, he was the son of an earl, so perhaps he really believed he was the catch of the year.

Politely, Celia let a few seconds pass, as though she were thinking over her answer. "Thank you, my lord, but…"

Wouldn't Simon just laugh at this? Two offers, and two almost-instant refusals. *At this rate, Silly,* he'd say, *you'll have run through the entire aristocracy by Boxing Day.*

Lord Billings drew himself up straight, heels clicking together. "Before you refuse me, Miss Overton, I should tell you that my sister will be along shortly."

He couldn't even propose marriage without help? "Then I beg you to consider, sir. You have made your offer and received my answer. That's the end of it, and there's no need to embarrass yourself by making the matter public."

He smiled. "You don't understand at all, my dear. It's not I who will be embarrassed. If you're foolish enough not to be agreeable, Hester will tell everyone she found us in a compromising position. With the resulting scandal threatening to ruin you – well, of course I shall do the gentlemanly thing and marry you. You may as well accept my offer right now."

Celia closed her book with a thump and tried to slide out of the window seat, but he moved to block her. He slid one arm around her and with his other hand pried her head up till she had to face him. "I suppose I shall have to," he said, almost to himself, and plastered his lips against hers. His mouth was wet and meaty.

The door creaked open again, and Lord Billings raised his head. "Hester?"

"Hardly," Simon said dryly. "I would ask for an explanation, Billings, but the situation seems clear."

"It's not what you think!" Desperately, Celia jammed the corner of her book into Lord Billings' stomach.

He shrieked and fell back, gripping his midsection as though she'd sliced him with a cleaver.

"Lord Billings is just leaving, Simon," she said coolly. "Though I fear he may need assistance to get to the door."

Simon leveled a stare at Lord Billings, who eyed him warily. Bent over and leaning on furniture as he went, the viscount stumbled out of the room.

Simon closed the door behind him. "You show promise as a bruiser, my dear – though I'd hate to see what he'd do if someone gave him a real jab in the belly. Are you all right?"

She felt safe with him in the room. Still, even though she nodded, Celia had started to tremble, and her voice shook. "He – he offered for me, and then threatened me when I refused him."

"That's something I didn't expect." Simon sat down beside her. "And obviously you didn't either, or you wouldn't have come off alone like this. Do you want me to take you home right now?"

Yes. But Celia Overton was made of sterner stuff than that. "We can't leave before the wedding. It would be too rude to Lady Stone."

Simon didn't seem to be listening. "Celia, my pet, that's quite a nice pair of silk garters you're wearing, but do you think you might pull your skirt down? I gather Hester's due to stop by any moment to catch you *in flagrante delicto*, and it might be as well if she didn't see me eyeing your underthings."

"Oh!" How had she not noticed that as she slid out of her cozy nook, trying to escape Lord Billings, her skirt had hiked up till her knees were exposed? How embarrassing that Simon had to tell her to get dressed properly!

Celia colored furiously and tugged her hem back into place. "Anyway, you know what will happen if I go home without being betrothed. Uncle Rupert will gloat over my failure and try yet again to match us up together."

Silence dropped over the room, stretching out like brittle threads of spun sugar.

"Would that be so terrible, Celia? At least we know each other's faults."

Her mouth dropped open. *Yes, we do,* she almost said. *And one of your faults, Simon Montrose, is that you're completely unromantic.* What a very depressing comedown it was, to receive an offer based on nothing more than practicality. "Honestly, Simon —"

Now her tally stood at three offers and three instant refusals. Could things get any more ridiculous?

"It would be a sensible match," Simon said. "And... well, have you really wanted anything – I mean anyone – you've met here?"

Dispiritedly, Celia shook her head. He was quite right that none of the gentlemen at Rockhill had made her heart trip even a tiny bit faster. But to go home defeated...

Tears threatened, but she blinked them back. "You're worried about your wager."

Simon handed her his handkerchief. "Well – not anymore."

She gave a spurt of a laugh. "Stop it! It's not fair that you can always make me smile, even when I'm feeling dejected."

The door swung open again and Lady Hester surged in. "I might have known," she began. "You've been trying to trap my brother since... *Simon*?"

Simon rose and bowed. "Were you expecting someone else to be here, Hester?"

She didn't answer but turned back toward the corridor to call, "He's in here."

Celia delicately wiped her eyes. His handkerchief smelled like Simon – a light, fresh mix of soap and sunshine and newly-cut grass.

A moment later one of the footmen appeared. "Mr. Montrose, a letter has come for you from Leicester." He held out a silver tray on which lay a folded sheet with wide black markings along every edge.

From home. Celia's breath caught. A letter marked in that way meant very bad news. But what sort of disaster could have struck them? "What is it, Simon?" Her breath caught. "Uncle Rupert? Not – oh, please – not my mother?"

Simon cracked the wafer and unfolded the page. A moment later, still staring at the letter, he said, "No. Both Uncle and your mother are safe; he merely sent the messenger straight on here. My cousin has died."

"Oh." She folded the handkerchief and held it out to him, but he didn't seem to notice. "I thought it was something important."

"The cousin who was Lord Montrose. And it seems I am next in line."

Celia groaned. "That's doing it up much too brown. Just because I was foolish enough to hint to the Carew sisters that you might someday have a title is no reason to tease me about it now. How did you find out what I told them, anyway?"

"Hester asked," he said absently. "I told her you were talking nonsense."

"As indeed I was. Why you think I would ever consider marrying you, Simon, when your greatest delight has always been to bamboozle me…"

He folded the letter and looked straight at her. "Perhaps because you'd be Lady Montrose?"

Celia's heart gave a strange little flutter. There was no glint of humor in Simon's eyes, no tenacious dimple, none of the signs that ordinarily warned her that he was cutting a wheedle.

She took the letter out of his hand and read it for herself.

With the death of an unknown relative and a few strokes of a pen, Simon had officially gained a title, presumably some sort of landed estate, a seat in the House of Lords… and the sort of eligibility in the marriage market that plain Mr. Montrose could only have longed hopelessly to achieve.

Simon Montrose. Viscount Montrose. My lord Montrose…

Celia swallowed hard and made her curtsy. "My lord." Her voice was raspy with strain.

She wondered how long it would take Lady Hester to break off her betrothal to Lord Lockwood, now that the man she so clearly preferred was eligible after all. Even if Simon still had – what was it the Carew sisters had called it? – a whiff of trade about him, when the daughter of an earl wed a viscount, society did not frown. The *ton* might even call it a brilliant match.

As indeed it is. He's a wonderful catch. But then he always was.

She sank down on the window seat once more, because her knees threatened to give way. A wonderful catch? How long had she thought of Simon in that way? And why had she never realized it?

You could have had him, Celia. Now it's too late.

If she had smiled at him just a few minutes ago and agreed to marry him after all, it would all be settled – because Simon would never go back on his word.

But she hadn't. Now if she even hinted that she'd changed her mind, he would believe it was because of his new circumstances. *You'd be Lady Montrose.*

He didn't really want to marry her anyway. His offer had been no more than a half-hearted attempt to console her. The best he'd been able to offer, the most promising thing about their potential union, was *At least we know each other's faults.* It was hardly the sort of thing a girl wanted to hear from her suitor.

Outside, the rain had stopped and the sky was growing light again. The storm had ended while she hadn't been paying attention – just as she hadn't paid attention as Simon crept into her heart.

When had he stopped being a tormenting annoyance and become the only man she could love?

At least now she understood why she had turned down Baron Draycott. It wasn't because his offer was unwelcome, or even because the man himself was a bore. She'd refused him because it had simply felt wrong to contemplate marriage with anyone who wasn't Simon.

There *had* been someone at the house party that she wanted. She wanted Simon. But she could never have him.

*****

After four consecutive evenings with the other ladies of the party, Simon had been looking forward to partnering Celia through their last dinner at Rockhill House. The girl might rear up like an excited colt when he teased her, but she was always entertaining.

But tonight she was quieter than he had ever seen her. It seemed as though someone had taken a painting in brilliant oils and covered it with muted, muddy chalk.

"Is Lord Bilious still bothering you?" he asked as he held her chair in the dining room. "I mean, are you fretting about what happened? – because if he were to dare approach you again, I'd knock him down."

She looked startled. "You would? No, of course it's not bothering me. I'm very grateful for your sense of timing, however. How did you happen to come in just then?"

"Something Hester said made me curious. I'm responsible for you, after all." He watched a shadow flicker in her eyes, and a lump settled in his chest. "Celia, I am most damnably sorry. I was very awkward. Can we just forget what I said this afternoon and go back to the way things used to be?"

"Forget…? Oh, *that*." She laughed. "I didn't take you seriously."

I noticed. "Then I haven't ruined everything?"

At the head of the table, Lord Stone cleared his throat and raised his glass. "To our newest peer – my lord Montrose."

The Carew sisters were all smiles – except when their gazes rested on Celia, sitting quietly beside him. Simon had to restrain the urge to slip a protective arm around her, to shield her from their acerbic looks.

When the table was cleared and the ladies left the dining room, he had to make an effort to enjoy the port. Lord Stone wanted to know details about the estate he'd inherited. Baron Draycott looked put out to find that Simon was suddenly his superior in the aristocratic hierarchy. Lord Lockwood maintained a stony, suspicious silence. Lord Tavish, apparently able to think for himself only because he was in a separate room from his bride, pestered to be told the history of the Montrose family and refused to believe Simon had heard only the sketchiest of versions. Lord Billings sat sipping a tisane brewed specially to coddle his stomach and stared venomously at Simon.

For the first time all week, he was delighted when it was time to rejoin the ladies.

Prudence waylaid him the moment he entered the drawing room, fluttering her fan and dropping *my lord* into her conversation almost at random. Simon barely listened, more interested in finding Celia – and he only relaxed when he saw her sitting with Lady Stone.

Prudence followed his gaze. "You may not have seen it, my lord, but it's clear to all of us that Miss Overton means to have you."

Her reasoning was completely asinine, of course. If she knew how very firmly he'd been rejected…

"Now that your situation has changed," she went on earnestly, "you need to be careful of her."

Or was it possible Prudence saw something he'd missed?

He let his gaze return to her, and smiled. "I shall, Miss Carew. You may be certain of it."

Tuesday

The morning of Imogene's wedding dawned clear and sunny, with the world washed clean of dust by the previous day's rainstorm. Celia was dressed early, ready for the walk to the village church where the wedding would take place. Rather than listen to the Carew sisters complaining about their hats and sashes and who-knew-what-else, she set her maid to finish her packing and walked out into the garden by herself.

In places, the foliage was still damp from the previous day's rain, but the graveled paths were dry enough if she kept to the center of them. It wasn't the scent of heliotrope drifting on the air which tugged at her senses, however; it was Simon's handkerchief, forgotten in the uproar over his letter. His scent on the linen was fainter now, but with any luck it might last a few days more.

She inhaled one last time and was tucking the folded square back into her sleeve as Simon called her name from the end of the garden. Her hand slipped and the handkerchief dropped to the gravel. She bent to snatch it up and tried in vain to hide it.

"Isn't that mine?" Simon asked.

"I couldn't find one of my own." What a foolish, unbelievable excuse – but it had popped out before Celia could think of anything better. "I thought it wise to have one at hand, in case I get emotional during the ceremony. Is it time?"

"Not yet. I wanted to talk to you, but you avoided me by going to bed early last night."

She didn't look at him. He was correct – but she had thought it unlikely he'd notice, with both Prudence and Dimity fawning over him. "I had a bit of a headache."

"So you said."

"If it is travel arrangements you want to discuss," she said quickly, "you need not trouble yourself over me. I have asked Lady Stone to send me home in her carriage, so you may take Uncle Rupert's."

Simon frowned. "Why?"

"Because when we came, you were on your way to Yorkshire – or had you forgotten? There's no need to trail back across England to escort me home and then make another trip to conduct your business."

"I wasn't planning to."

She looked at him sharply. "Oh? I suppose now you're a landed gentleman, you'll be leaving Uncle Rupert to deal with everything on his own?"

"You're a bit of a shrew this morning."

Celia bit her lip. "I'm sorry. That was very harsh of me. You have new responsibilities to consider."

"It's my current responsibility which weighs on my mind, Celia. I do regret what I said yesterday."

The words were like a rasp scraping her skin. Of course he regretted offering for her – now that his situation had changed. "It was perfectly clear you felt sorry for me. But you needn't. Perhaps I'll still accept the baron."

Simon frowned. "He offered for you? Why haven't you answered him?"

Celia cursed her wayward tongue. Was she trying to prove to him that she wasn't completely undesirable after all? Or that she could have won their wager, had she chosen?

"I answered," she said slowly. "I said no."

He stretched out a hand and kept her from turning away from him. "Why, Celia?"

"It doesn't matter. I only told you because you shouldn't have felt you must offer for me – particularly now that you could have Hester after all."

"Why would I want her?"

His question – simple and straightforward – struck Celia like a blow. "You don't want her?"

"Good God, no. As soon as she began to hint that my suit might be welcome after all, I ended it."

"After the letter came yesterday, you mean?"

"No. Weeks ago."

"But she came to your bedroom after the ball." She colored a little. "I… happened to walk by."

"You thought I'd invited her to spend the night with me? No. In fact, I wasn't there. She must have waited a while before she left a note saying she needed to speak with me. I think she was hoping I'd be so shocked at the news of her betrothal that I'd declare myself."

"*Hester*?"

"I'm convinced her father isn't as well off as he wants the world to believe. An infusion of cash might be exactly the ticket to save the earldom. But since I don't care to be married for money, either mine or Uncle Rupert's…"

"Do you think that's why Viscount Billings tried to compromise me?"

Simon nodded. "Not that you aren't enchanting enough to tempt a man, but I don't think Lord Bilious is that man."

"Cut line, Simon – you don't think I'm enchanting."

"That's a bad habit of yours, my dear. Telling me what I think."

Celia frowned.

"Have I really ruined things by offering for you?"

She hesitated, then nodded. It was true, after all; his offer had changed everything, for she would never again be able to look on him as simply another member of the family. The fact that she'd fallen in love with him was immaterial.

"Then I have nothing to lose. Will you marry me, Celia?"

For a moment she thought she couldn't have heard him correctly. "Right now you're just feeling hunted, so settling down with someone you've known forever must seem the sensible course of action."

"That's mostly right," he admitted, "even if you are once more telling me what I think. I've always expected that someday, when I was ready, I'd marry you."

"Because Uncle Rupert wanted it? How very flattering."

"It's not romantic, I know – but it's the honest truth, Celia. You've always been a familiar and comfortable part of my life, and I couldn't imagine it being any other way. I thought it was likely that someday we'd have a familiar and comfortable marriage."

Her head was spinning. "Then why did you wager that I could marry someone else?"

Simon shrugged. "Because you made it clear you didn't feel the same way I did. You wanted a different kind of man, and I wanted you to be happy. But then we came here and I saw you in an entirely new light."

"Instead of as part of the furniture?" Celia knew she sounded tart, but she didn't care.

"I'm not saying this very well, am I?"

"You could use practice before you go out into the Marriage Mart, yes."

"Very well." He took a deep breath. "You weren't just Celia anymore. I saw the way the gentlemen reacted to you, and I listened to them talk about your glorious hair and your wonderful laugh."

"They did? What else did they say?"

He bit back a smile. "Celia, I'm trying to woo you here, but if you'd rather I tell you what every other man at this party thinks of you... That's one of the things I love, you know – the fact that you so seldom do or say or think what I expect."

Love? She wasn't certain she'd heard right.

"I was amused at first, and shamefully slow to realize what was happening – even though I found myself wanting to push all of them away and tell them you were mine. I never expected to find myself feeling romantic about a girl I've known since pigtail days, so I didn't realize I was experiencing good old-fashioned jealousy."

"Over me?" Her voice was little more than a breath.

"Over you, Celia. As it turns out, it's always been you. Your hair *is* glorious and your laugh *is* wonderful, but that's not what I love. It's your sharp sense of humor and the fact that you're a lady without being in the least stuffy about it. And then there's your infectious giggle – the one that makes me smile even when I most want to wring your neck."

"Why didn't you say something?"

"Because it wouldn't have been fair to you to interfere, not to let you make your own choice. I really did try to stand back and let you get to know them all." He brushed a tendril of hair back from her face with a gentle hand. "But also I was afraid to tell you what I'd discovered in my own heart. Afraid you didn't feel the same way, because telling you I'd fallen in love with you would mean we could never go back to that old, easy way we had."

"That *old, easy way* where you felt entitled to tease the life out of me?"

"Guilty – but you did laugh when Uncle Rupert suggested we might marry."

She couldn't deny it. Only now did she recall the odd, fleeting expression which had crossed Simon's face when she giggled at the very idea. "Is *that* how you look when you want to wring my neck? I'll have to remember."

"Very wise of you to make a note of it. When I finally did speak, I made you a dry, chilly, practical, sensible offer, instead of telling you that I've fallen madly in love."

"Simon Montrose as a romantic figure? I'm too stunned to take it all in, I think."

"Am I being foolish, Celia? You haven't answered me."

Celia was so euphoric she was having trouble drawing a full breath, but she kept her voice calm. "Perhaps Lady Stone is a fairy godmother, after all. There must have been something magical going on this week, for both of us to suddenly see the truth in ways we never could before. In ways we might never have recognized if not for this party." She looked up at him. "I had no idea until we came here that it's you I love, Simon. You're the only man I could ever love."

Simon took her hands and drew her close. She gasped as his arms closed around her, but willingly lifted her face for his kiss.

His mouth was soft against hers, gentle rather than demanding, and then as she responded he asked for more and she willingly gave it. She'd had no idea a kiss could be like this – hot and all-consuming, tasting of summertime and ale, promising delights and making her wonder how long it would be before they could be married.

Lady Stone's gravelly voice broke through Celia's warm sensual haze. "Are you two almost finished?"

Celia's squeak was the only sound she was capable of making. How had she ended up leaning against a tree, feeling rumpled and confused and out of breath and entirely wonderful, with Simon's breath warm against her throat and his lips even warmer against... *Oh, my.*

She tried to push him away, but she might as well have attempted to move one of the century-old oaks along Rockhill's carriage drive. She turned her head, saw the absorbed crowd lined up on the path – the Carew sisters looked particularly out of sorts – and buried her face in Simon's shoulder.

"We've only started, ma'am," Simon said calmly. "You go ahead to the wedding, and we'll catch up in a few minutes." He turned his back to the onlookers, shielding Celia from view. He kissed her hair, found her ear and traced it with the tip of his tongue, ran his fingers across her nape. "It's safe to come out now. They're gone."

She peeked first, before she raised her head.

"You're right about the magic," he said. "The party, the wedding, being away from home, being thrown together. I know I laughed at the idea of Lady Stone as some sort of fairy godmother – "

"You called her a witch," Celia reminded.

"Did I? I shall have to apologize." He kissed her again, long and thoroughly. "We really should go, or we'll miss the wedding." He took her hand and laid it on his arm, covering her fingers possessively with his own.

"You know what the worst of it's going to be?" Celia said thoughtfully.

"I suppose that for the rest of my life you'll be trying to tell me what I think, whether it's how I like my breakfast eggs or how to raise our children."

Children... The thought of a couple of sons to inherit Simon's bent for mischief, along with a little girl for the boys to tease, sent a tiny thrill through her. "That's not what I meant, though of course you'll torment me and I'll be annoyed about it."

"You get as bristly as a hairbrush. I find it captivating."

She decided to ignore him. "The unbearable bit is going to be Uncle Rupert crowing about being right."

"No doubt. Though as it happens, you can always throw up to him that you did exactly what you said you'd do. You're coming home as the promised bride of a titled gentleman."

Her eyes widened. "That's right! I won my bet. Pay up, Simon."

"You only managed to win by bending the rules."

"Make it a wedding gift?" she said softly, and he stopped in the middle of the path to kiss her again. A long while later, he said unsteadily, "If you can put up with Uncle Rupert crowing about his triumph, so can I – because we belong together, Silly. Forever."

And for perhaps the first time in her life, Celia found herself in complete agreement with him.

Epilogue

Stone House, London

To: Mr. Rupert Overton

I hope you're satisfied with the outcome of my little house party, Rupert, though I must admit I am not. I became fond of Celia and I hoped she would catch my nephew's eye and put the common sense you're so proud of to good use in preserving his riches.

But of course it was not to be. You got your wish, and I did not get mine. Not that I fault Celia's judgment, for young Lord Montrose - as I suppose you will forever resist calling him - would have been a catch even without a title. Or for that matter, even without your money.

I suppose you'll think my comment is heresy, Rupert, but though I may be old, I'm far from blind. He is a handsome and virile young man —

But I have allowed myself to be distracted. The point, old friend, is that you are now obliged to me. I've done as you asked and shaken the scales from the eyes of your young relatives. Now it's your turn. What are we going to do about that nephew of mine?

Yours sincerely,

Lucinda, Lady Stone

An Affair for the Season

-1-

Always before, the notes from her lover had been delivered discreetly – though as the Season began to wind down and Julia's time in London grew shorter, the messages had occasionally come in unexpected ways. The one thing she'd never anticipated, however, was to sit down at the breakfast table, flip through her morning's post, and find a letter addressed to her in the slashing black handwriting which had become so familiar in the last few weeks.

Julia drew a quick breath at the sight, and across the table her husband looked up from his newspaper with faint interest. "Is something wrong, ma'am? Not bad news, I hope?"

"Of course not. I…" She coughed, hoping to imply that she'd merely swallowed wrongly.

Lord Sherwood's gaze dropped back to his newspaper. "I see Stilwell created another dust-up in the Commons yesterday. I suppose it'll have to be discussed in the Lords."

"Will you be going to the chamber, sir?" She kept her voice casual as she slipped James's note out of the stack of letters, tucking it under her knee where the frilly skirt of her morning dress, draped over the seat of her chair, would conceal it. Foolish, perhaps, to think her husband would take any interest in her letters. She shouldn't have reacted without thinking. But now that she'd hidden the note, she couldn't exactly bring it out again without drawing his attention. She supposed she'd simply have to sit here, toying with her toast, until Sherwood left the table.

"Just as I always do, yes." He turned a page. "And what is your plan for the day? More shopping with your friends?"

Not knowing what James's note said made it difficult to give a sensible answer, so Julia chose to be vague. "I haven't decided. One does become weary of the shops."

"You'd best take advantage of the opportunity. The business of the House of Lords seems likely to adjourn today, and I've a mind to return to Everleigh immediately. Tomorrow, in fact."

She couldn't stop herself from responding. "So soon?"

His gaze sharpened. "A moment ago you said you were weary of the shops."

"But I am not weary of London, sir."

"Only yesterday you seemed to be longing to see our son."

The mere reminder of her baby, that small and delightful bundle who snuggled so confidingly against her, made Julia's heart ache. But he was at Everleigh with his nurse, who was confident that a mother was an unnecessary complication in an infant's life. "Well, of course I miss him. I wish we'd brought him with us." She brightened. "We *could* direct his nurse to bring him to London after all."

Sherwood had focused on his newspaper again. "The city is no place for an infant. It will be far easier for us to go home. Have your maid start packing today."

With relief, Julia remembered the best of all possible excuses. "I can't miss Lady Stone's ball, for I promised her I would attend."

"Because she assured you that anyone who doesn't make an appearance at her event will most certainly regret it?"

Had Sherwood read her mind? Those were the exact words the elderly Lady Stone had used. Julia shivered at the idea that he might be eavesdropping on her thoughts, and then realized what must have happened instead. "That sounds very much as if you, too, have encountered her."

"Yesterday, just outside my club – on a street no true lady would walk down, so of course Lady Stone was there." He folded the newspaper and laid it aside. "Anything you and Lady Stone agree on, a mere male cannot stand against. Very well, ma'am. I won't tear you away until after Lady Stone's ball."

Relief flickered along Julia's nerves – foolish though it was to feel that way. One ball more or less, a few days one way or the other, could make no real difference. Her Season and her affair were coming to an end.

Sherwood looked at her sharply, as if he'd caught her reaction. "I didn't realize, however, that you and Lady Stone were such bosom friends."

Julia shrugged. "You've often said that for an old gossip, Lady Stone wields an enormous amount of power in the *ton*."

"And so she does." He rose from his chair. "Your reminder that it is unwise to cross her is a timely one." He bent over her for a moment, and Julia's stomach went tight. But he merely dropped a casual brush of the lips atop the lacy matron's cap that covered her dark hair. "However, the day after Lady Stone's ball, we are off for home."

"The very day after? But the ball might run into the early morning hours, and…"

"You can rest in the carriage, and all summer in the country," he said crisply. "I shall see you at dinner. Always assuming the Lords do not end the session by sitting late tonight."

"Of course," Julia said. She picked at her toast until she heard the front door close behind him. She glanced around warily, making certain that the butler hadn't come silently into the breakfast room, before she retrieved her lover's note and cracked the wax seal.

Today, outside your milliner's shop, at eleven.

There was no signature, but she didn't need one. And though there was also not a flourish or a romantic overtone or an endearment, there was a very practical reason for that omission. Messages had a habit of going astray, especially when they must pass through multiple sets of hands – often from James's groom to hers, then through a footman or a maid before finally reaching Julia herself. Even her own lady's maid was trustworthy only up to a point.

She tucked the note inside her slipper, under the arch of her foot. Later, when she was alone, she'd extract it and put it away in the small secret compartment at the bottom of her jewel case, to keep company with the others she had collected in the weeks since their affair began.

Breathless and exciting and unforgettable weeks...

Up in her bedroom, Julia found her maid straightening the dressing table. "Help me into my pink walking dress, please, Mary. I'm going out to see the milliner."

The maid looked startled, as well she might. Donning the newest and most flattering of her dresses for a mere errand to a tradesman? "Shall you want me to come with you, my lady?"

"Not this time. Lord Sherwood wishes you to begin packing, for we return to Everleigh no later than the end of the week. Put my new bonnet in a hat box, please. I'm taking it back."

The maid looked puzzled. "But you seemed so happy with it when it was delivered, my lady."

"I noticed yesterday that it has a loose bit of trim."

"Couldn't I fix that, ma'am, and save you the errand?"

"I have no doubt you could, Mary, but since the bonnet has not yet been worn, it seems the milliner should attend to her own carelessness." Julia pulled off her lace cap and let her long dark brown hair tumble around her shoulders.

"Yes, ma'am." Mary picked up the hairbrush. As Julia met her maid's gaze in the mirror, she saw a sudden conspiratorial gleam spring to life there.

She knows, Julia thought.

-2-

Her affair with James had begun simply enough –
almost accidentally, in fact, or at least she told herself so
– at the ball given by the Earl and Countess of
Summersby to introduce their daughter to the *ton*. The
Season had already gotten off to a good start, and the
Summersbys' house in Berkeley Square was crowded
with girls just out of the schoolroom. When Julia's
dance card didn't immediately fill, she wasn't entirely
surprised.

Midway through the evening, James had bowed
before her and asked for her card, signing his name
with that black slash which had since become so
familiar. When it was time for their waltz he swept her
across the floor with such skill and grace that she
allowed herself to stop thinking and just enjoy the
music and the movement and the sheer pleasure of
dancing with someone who was so very good at
guiding her through the steps and the crowd. So
perhaps she hadn't been quite as much on guard as a
married lady ought to be, and perhaps she had allowed
him to hold her more closely than was proper.

Still, she had been taken aback when, barely a
minute into the dance, he'd observed, "You seem sad
tonight. What a shame it is, when the most beautiful
lady in the room feels blue."

"You flatter me, sir. But then, you always did."

His smile gleamed and his eyes sparkled, and the
expression brought Julia's thoughts back to the days of
her own first London Season. James had been one of a
half-dozen gentlemen who had paid particular attention
to her, and there was no denying he'd been the most
charming man to be found anywhere in the *ton* that
year. All the girls thought so – and with good reason,
Julia reminded herself. She couldn't recall even one he
hadn't flirted with.

"It is not flattery to tell the truth, my lady. Is your unhappiness because the young men are now standing in line for the new debutantes instead of for you?" His deep voice tickled her ears.

Julia laughed. "I am scarcely so shallow as that, sir. I had my turn."

"Indeed you did, and you showed the world how it should be done. It would be no surprise if you look back fondly on the days of your own first Season, when many of those same men hovered around you like a swarm of –"

She interrupted pertly. "Like a swarm of flies around a sweat-slickened horse?"

His smile was both beautiful and infectious. "I was going to say, a swarm of bees around the sweetest honey to be found in all England. Tell me truly – are you missing the days when you were the acknowledged beauty, the Incomparable?"

If she hadn't been looking into his compelling dark eyes, she might have uttered the socially-acceptable answer. But his gaze seemed to reach inside her and tug, and she whispered, "Yes. Yes, I am."

Until that moment, she hadn't even admitted to herself that she felt jealous of this year's new crop of girls, or acknowledged that she was just a little downcast because the course of her life was laid out so clearly. Her husband's heir was safely in his nursery at Everleigh, fawned over and attended by an entire staff of nannies and maids under the direction of the best baby nurse in England. Sherwood was occupied by estate matters, which seemed to take a great deal of attention. Julia was left with no real role except to run her husband's country house, but the housekeeper and butler had been entrenched long before she had come to Everleigh. They had everything so firmly in hand that she seldom interfered.

Julia had looked forward to coming back to London, after she'd spent the whole of last year's Season at Everleigh because she was increasing. But now that she was actually here, the experience wasn't what she'd expected at all. Sherwood's politics kept him occupied; she'd come to realize that his involvement in the House of Lords was the only real reason they were in the city. Her family was far away. Her friends had their own entertainments, and though she was always welcome to join them, the way they spent their days seemed every bit as trivial and uninspiring as her own pastimes.

She and James made another turn of the floor in silence, which gave her plenty of time to regret speaking her mind – no matter how true her words had been.

Then he said quietly, "I perceive that you miss the excitement and adventure of the unknown. But there is another way to have that excitement – that adventure – and even more."

She frowned. "What do you suggest I do, sir?"

He drew her closer. "Take a lover."

She was too startled to answer for a moment. "I'm a married woman. I have a child!"

He smiled. "But of course; I should hardly suggest it otherwise. Your husband is very focused on his responsibilities. Is it not true that he spends all his days in the House of Lords, and a good many of his nights as well?"

"His sense of duty is not for me to criticize."

"But you may as well admit it, my lady. You're just a bit bored."

She didn't answer directly. "It's true I miss my baby."

He smiled again. "*Only* your baby? You could not have said anything which would make me more certain I am right, you know. You have fulfilled your responsibility by giving your husband his heir. He entertains himself with politics. Why should he mind if you entertain yourself with a lover?"

"Do you fancy yourself some sort of doctor, so lightly prescribing an *affaire*?"

"A doctor of the heart, if you like," James said. "And I do not mean just any casual lover. I suggest you choose me."

She actually laughed, showing such delight that a nearby couple stared at them in surprise, and the waltz ended just then. James swept her an elegant bow, flashed his beautiful smile, and released her to the gentleman who was to partner her in the next country dance.

Julia walked through the figures in a daze. What madness it was even to contemplate such a thing – and yet she could think of nothing but what he had suggested. Even though James was across the room, she knew precisely where he stood and exactly when he looked in her direction. His deep voice still teased her ears, his touch still warmed her, his cologne still lingered where her hands had brushed against him. Her fingertips itched to reach up and smooth back the unruly curl which had tumbled over his brow as they waltzed.

He left her alone for most of the evening but claimed the final waltz before the ball ended. "Two waltzes in one evening," she said as they took the floor. "Sir, I must warn you that the gossips will notice."

"I doubt it. I believe they are focused on this Season's Incomparable instead."

"It is cruel of you to suggest that I am now invisible to the *ton*, sir." She tried to inject a note of humor in her voice.

Clearly he noticed both the effort and her failure. "Adventure," he said softly. "Excitement. That is what I offer – a bit of spice to liven up an otherwise ordinary Season. Your friends may be excited by gambling more than they can afford, but I hardly think that would amuse you. Or they entertain themselves by buying gowns and hats and bagatelles, or in flirting."

"Everyone flirts, in the *ton*." She caught herself. "I mean—"

He smiled. "Then there can be no harm in you flirting with me. For right now, if you wish, we shall confine ourselves to that innocent pastime. But I have been honest about my desires, and should you decide to take my advice—"

"I need only crook my finger to summon you?"

"No, my lady." His voice was husky. "I will read your change of heart in your eyes. You surely will not hold it against me if I hope for more than simple flirting?"

She was too startled to answer, but he seemed to take her lack of response as assent, for he guided her toward a deserted corner of the ballroom. The moment the waltz ended, they were out of sight of the dancers in a small alcove set off by velvet curtains.

He raised her face to his and kissed her slowly, his lips firm but gentle.

"I can't think this is—" she began.

"Don't think. Only feel." He traced the outline of her lips with the tip of his tongue, and something curled into life deep inside her, hot and heavy and willing. There had always been something about James which made her wish to fling common sense to the winds...

He's not really serious. It's only a flirtation, nothing more.

He seemed to feel her reservations relax, for his tongue slipped between her lips and sampled her deeply. He tasted of the brandy he must have been drinking while she danced away the evening, and the mellow unexpectedness of it sent heat through her. She was as unsteady as if she'd spent the last few hours sipping from a snifter herself, and as her knees went weak he gathered her closer yet.

"You see, I want more," he whispered against her lips, and she could feel the hard bulge of his erection against her belly. "You must set the pace, my sweet, for I would have no qualms about taking you right now."

"Here?" she squeaked. "I don't even know how you'd—"

He smiled. "Are you asking me to tell you or to show you?" His voice was low and mesmerizing, the deep tones caressing her ears.

"No!" Julia braced her hands against his chest, and though he did not let her go, he loosened his grasp so she could stand a few inches away from him. Her breath caught in her throat. "I should return to the ballroom," she said uncertainly.

He didn't stop her. Leaving him behind, she emerged from the curtains expecting that everyone who saw her would instantly know what she'd been doing. But though she felt as though she'd been hidden away in that seductive little corner forever, only a few minutes had passed, and the company was still forming for the last country dance of the evening. Her next partner presented himself – and a good thing it was that she'd reappeared before he'd come looking for her, too.

He looked curious, however, so though Julia thought longingly for a moment of the refreshment room and something very cold to restore her equilibrium, she gave up the idea almost immediately. Sitting out the dance would mean carrying on a sensible conversation, something she was by no means certain she could do. Instead, she threw herself into the complex and demanding figures, seizing the excuse of the dance in case she appeared flushed and tousled and not quite herself.

The music went on and on, and with every turn and swirl and pass through the lines of dancers, she found herself watching for James – and finding him on the sidelines, his dark gaze fixed on her.

When she got home that evening, she slipped her dance card into the secret compartment in the bottom of her jewel case. It was the first time since her debut that she'd kept such a sentimental trinket.

-3-

After the Summersbys' ball, Julia could think of nothing but James and that sudden, confusing – and oh, so tempting! – invitation.

The day after the ball was her regular afternoon to be at home to callers, and she wondered if he might actually appear in her drawing room. But that would be too obvious, she told herself. Gentlemen clustered around the belles who were in their first Season, or else they spent their time with their male cohorts. They did not pay formal calls on married ladies – at least not without drawing the attention of the gossips. And surely James had more sense than to court that sort of notice.

So Julia chattered with her friends, many of whom she had met during her own first Season. Most of the ladies in her group were married now; the few acquaintances who had not yet found matches were busy making calls and friends among the fresh crop of debutantes instead.

The ladies swapped gossip and shared tidbits about where to find the most elegant hats and the sheerest stockings. But their chatter all seemed perfectly ordinary to Julia. Their world of pilfering maids and annoying housekeepers and troublesome footmen and petty friends was so much less interesting that the possibility of a secret, torrid affair.

Not that she would actually do anything more than flirt, of course. How embarrassing it would have been if someone else had stumbled through those curtains last night and found them in that little alcove! – even though they'd only been kissing. As for the idea of anything more – well, the space had been too tiny even for a chair. How James could have considered actually making love there… Julia's mind boggled. Every possibility she considered seemed even more impossible and more outlandish than the last.

What she should have done, she decided in the end, was to challenge him. He simply couldn't have carried out his sultry promise, and that would have been the end of it. Though it would have been a shame if she had embarrassed him enough to make him retreat entirely. Flirting – so long as it was *only* flirting, of course – might be fun.

It seemed, however, that wherever Julia chose to spend her evenings, James did not. A few days later, in the midst of a musicale, she found herself tuning out the dreadful wail of an amateur violinist and thinking instead about James. "I will read your change of heart in your eyes," he had said. But what a hum that was, since he could hardly judge her expression when he wasn't even in the same room.

As soon as she admitted to herself that once again he was not going to make an appearance, Julia found herself restless and out of sorts – even though she laughed at her own silliness in having taken him seriously for even a moment. He'd been talking nonsense, that was all, but she had to admit he'd entertained her so thoroughly that for a few days – while she thought over that flattering proposition – she'd forgotten her boredom entirely.

She had just made up her mind that it was time to settle back into her normal routine and stop giving a thought to James when she looked up, her eyes practically watering from the horrible screeching of the violin, and caught his eye across the room. For a moment, she couldn't look away, even though she could feel herself turning delicately, embarrassingly pink under his languid survey. Her insides had gone all aflutter just from seeing him, even before he let his gaze wander slowly over her entire body – and James, the bounder, clearly knew it.

He hadn't even crossed the room to speak to her. But the next morning, her lady's maid brought a note along with her morning chocolate, setting their first assignation for that afternoon, along Rotten Row.

She shouldn't go, of course. She shouldn't appear to have been waiting for his summons – and it *was* a summons; his note had contained almost an air of command.

She scolded herself as she ordered her mare to be saddled. And again as she got into her riding habit and made certain that every draping fold was properly brushed and her bonnet was perched at the most flattering angle. And yet again as she allowed the stable boy to help her into the saddle, and as she trotted off toward the park with her groom trailing behind.

Her horse had barely set a hoof onto Rotten Row when James pulled his rangy gelding up alongside her. "You are exactly on time, my sweet. Does that mean you were eager to see me?"

"I beg your pardon?" she said carelessly. "Were you expecting me, sir? I ride every afternoon unless I am receiving callers or taking the air with a friend in a carriage. I would be here whether you were or not."

He smiled. "How thoughtful of you to arrange things so that I need not send frequent notes and risk them being put into the wrong hands! I shall look forward to our regular meetings in the park."

Julia blinked in amazement. Exactly how had he turned her simple statement back on her, making it seem as though *she* was the one inviting a daily tryst along Rotten Row?

She felt breathless, out of her depth – and for the first time since his madcap proposition, she wondered if embarking on even the simplest of flirtations with James might not be quite safe.

Riding casually beside her, completely relaxed as he nodded greetings to acquaintances as they passed, James matched the pace of Julia's mare precisely and effortlessly. But in the press of horses and riders, he edged closer, and the white cuff of his topboot brushed against the soft dark blue wool of her riding habit. For just an instant, his knee pressed against hers. The simple touch sent a thrill through her, and Julia caught her breath.

Though he couldn't possibly have heard that tiny gasp, James turned his head to look at her, and the warmth and desire in his eyes melted her stomach into a puddle. "I assume you'll be attending Lady Stone's next soiree, ma'am."

"And dinner beforehand." She didn't quite know why she said it.

"Then I shall see you there." He didn't touch her again, but as they rode along, he chatted easily. About flowers, of all things – or at least, a casual eavesdropper would believe he was discussing botany. Julia knew, however, that as he described stroking silken petals and sniffing delicate scents, he was thinking of … other things.

She tried not to listen to his nonsense, but her body seemed to have its own ideas. As he talked, she went all slack and soft and warm and moist, as though every note of his rich, deep voice was a caress against her bare skin. Her breathing acquired a hitch – not exactly painful, but her chest was tight with anticipation. Her mouth was dry, though for a moment she thought she could actually still taste the warm richness of his brandy from their kiss days ago. The sensation left her feeling a bit dizzy, unfocused, and she had to concentrate to keep her mare under control.

"My lady," he said finally. "Am I disturbing you?"

Julia would never admit it, though she was afraid her voice would rasp when she tried to speak. "I don't understand why you're doing this."

"You mean, why am I trying to seduce you?"

She looked around quickly, hoping no one was close enough to overhear.

"My sweet, you must realize I've been mad for you since the first time we met." His voice was low and held not even a quiver of amusement. "My fondest dream on that day was to take you as my lover."

"Despite the fact that you flirted with every young woman within range?"

"Oh, but that was only to disguise from prying eyes the way I felt about you. This – our affair – is inevitable, you know. It has been since the day I first laid eyes on you."

Julia quirked an eyebrow at him. "You're so certain of yourself, sir, that your confidence borders on arrogance."

"With good reason, I believe – for surely you've noticed that nothing is keeping you beside me. All you need do is snap your fingers for your groom and ride away home, and I should be properly put in my place. Yet here you stay – beside me."

"I choose not to cheat myself of the afternoon air."

He laughed outright at that, and nearby a matron looked around as though surprised to hear such rich enjoyment.

Julia ducked her head. She had to admit her quick excuse had been thoroughly feeble. "In any case, a ride in the park is not…"

He nodded. "I quite agree. It's not at all the same as a romp in b—"

"This is a public place," she said between clenched teeth. "You cannot say such things."

"Nothing's stopping me from thinking them, however – and clearly you are thinking along similar lines, or you wouldn't recognize and object to my thoughts."

She felt guilty color wash over her cheeks.

"But I shall bend to your ladylike desires and leave the subject – for now." James was as good as his word, and moved on to more general subjects. The *ton*, the upcoming parties, the horse he'd seen at Tattersall's that morning…

Not that it mattered. Whatever he chose to talk about, Julia could barely take her gaze off his lips. If he had sat down to read to her from Burke's *Peerage*, with all its dry recitations of who had sired whom for the last five hundred years, the caress of his voice would have still left her itchy with the desire to be touched. She shifted restlessly in her saddle and the friction of her movement focused her awareness on the warm, damp place between her legs. She was paying no attention at all to her mare, relying on the horse's good sense to keep her pacing along beside James's roan.

"My lady?" James said politely. "Do I weary you with my chatter?"

Julia jerked the reins as she pulled her mind back to the path, realizing that his eyes were alight with laughter. *Time to put him in his place.* Even the most exhilarating flirt couldn't be allowed to think he was so entertaining that he needn't even *try*. "Well, yes – a bit."

"Then I shall be happy to translate my words into actions."

She bit her tongue. That hadn't gone at all as she'd expected. "But I must not selfishly keep you beside me, sir. In any case, it is time for me to return home." She looked around for her groom.

"It shall be my pleasure to escort you," James said softly.

He stayed beside her all the way back to Bruton Street and the Sherwood town house, with her groom trailing dutifully behind. At the front door James dismounted to lift her down from her saddle. Though she'd thought perhaps he would take advantage of that moment of intimacy, he assisted her in much the same way as any gentleman would have – until he leaned closer and whispered, "I shall be waiting for our next encounter, at Lady Stone's soiree."

The phrase was almost innocuous, but his tone was not – and considering the way Julia's knees went weak, he might as well have been whispering an invitation to make love on Lady Stone's dining room table.

James waited in the street until she had climbed the steps and been admitted by the footman stationed at the entrance – a footman who cast a puzzled look at her, Julia thought, as he closed the great front door behind her – and then he rode away. She wondered where he was going.

-4-

As Lady Stone's dinner guests gathered in her drawing room, James didn't seek Julia out, so they hadn't yet exchanged a word when the dinner gong sounded. Since it turned out that he was assigned to be Lady Bellingham's dinner partner, there would be no opportunity to converse during the meal either.

That was just as well, Julia thought, for if James had a couple of hours to whisper nonsense into her ear, she would probably have burst into flames by the time the sweet was brought in. This way she would be able to thoroughly enjoy dinner without having to be on guard all the time.

She told herself she was quite glad of it – until she found herself sitting directly across the table from him. Though he spent the entire meal conversing in turn with the lady on each side of him, it seemed to Julia that he never quite took his gaze off her. Each time he lifted his wine glass, he subtly saluted her. Now and then he sent the tiniest of smiles her way – smiles so fleeting and casual that no one else would notice, or they would think his amusement arose from some humorous comment made by his dinner partner. But Julia knew those smiles were meant for her alone.

The entire dinner party served as a wordless slow-motion seduction, leaving her absolutely uncertain of what – or whether – she'd swallowed, except for suspecting she'd drunk more wine than was good for her. By the time the ladies withdrew, Julia was feeling a bit giddy and high-strung and almost dizzy. Rather than trying to settle herself amongst the crowd of late-arriving guests who were being ushered up to the drawing room, she made an excuse – something foolish about attending to a spot on her skirt – and tiptoed out against the press of guests who were climbing the stairs to join the soiree.

Down the hall from the drawing room, a door stood ajar. She vaguely recalled a music room there – though why Lady Stone even had such a thing, when she was clearly the least musical female in the *ton*, was more than Julia cared to contemplate.

As she passed the darkened room, she saw a shadow move in the dimness inside, and an instant later a hand closed on her arm and tugged her gently through the doorway. James pushed the door closed, and she was in his arms before she could take a breath – though she wasn't certain whether he had captured her or she had flung herself at him.

His lips and his hands were everywhere, hot, seeking, demanding. "Admit it," he said against her mouth. "You've been waiting all evening for this – as have I." His lips traveled slowly down her throat, nipping and licking and tasting, until he'd freed her breast from the low-cut dinner gown and slowly drew her nipple into his mouth. She pressed against him, moaning.

He smiled and drew her closer, cupping his hands over her derriere and pulling her tight against him till the heat and hardness of his erection nestled closely against her belly. Even through the layers of fabric which separated them, she could feel his urgency, and his voice sounded slightly hoarse.

Julia seized the last remnants of her common sense. "We can't. Not here. Lady Stone is one of my oldest friends."

"She's old, certainly," James said dryly. "And she fully understands how the *ton* works. If she was not in the mood to wink at indiscretion, she'd have locked this room." He nibbled once more at her breast. "There's a very nice settee over by the fire. Would you care to join me there?"

"She's the worst gossip in London, James!"

"What an odd thing to say about a woman you consider one of your oldest friends. Still, I have never known Lady Stone to pass along idle talk about people she likes." He drew her down next to him on the settee and nuzzled her breast.

"I can't do this... not in my friend's house!" Even as Julia protested, however, she arched her back and pushed her nipple more deeply into his mouth.

"You already are *doing this*, my sweet," he whispered. Somehow his hand had slid under her skirt and he found his way unerringly past the top of her silk stocking, past the bow of her garter ribbon, to the soft and sensitive skin of her thigh, and higher. He brushed the slit in her drawers and found the curls between her legs, and he caught her gasp against his mouth as he slipped a fingertip inside her. "But very well," he said, and paused. "If you can't, you can't."

Unable to control herself, she thrust her hips forward, taking his finger more deeply inside her. He laughed and began to play with her – gently thrusting and exploring, then backing off and tantalizing her with feathery touches, then settling into rhythmic strokes – until she was so lost to herself that she climaxed with a force which threatened to shatter her.

He smothered her cry with a hard kiss and held her close, stroking and petting her, until her quivering stopped and she lay passive in his arms. She was too embarrassed to quite meet his gaze, because doing so would confirm that nothing like this had ever happened to her before. Perhaps it was the secret, forbidden nature of their tryst, but she had never before felt a pleasure that was quite so intense and so unforgettable.

She reached up to brush the errant curl back from his forehead, and then she let her hand wander almost hesitantly across his elegant black coat and down over the slick satin of his knee breeches, the garb that the matrons of the *ton* insisted was the only appropriate thing for a gentleman to wear to dinner.

He captured her hand just as she was about to cup his erection, and kissed her temple gently. "Not just now."

"But you..."

"For this moment, my satisfaction lies in giving you release. Besides, you have been absent from the ladies for too long as it is."

For a few minutes she had entirely forgotten she was in Lady Stone's music room – with her lover. How, Julia asked herself, could she have lost herself so completely, forgetting her surroundings because of something as simple as the touch of his hand?

James helped her stand and smoothed her skirt back into place, tightened the laces at her back, adjusted the frill at the edge of her bodice. He was as expert as a lady's maid at putting her back together, though to tell the truth there wasn't any real damage to repair. He hadn't even mussed her hair or disarranged a bow. And clearly *he* hadn't forgotten for an instant where they were, or how easy it would be for someone to hear them, for he had even anticipated that she would call out in pleasure and had prevented her from giving them away.

Obviously, she thought, he was a very experienced lover. For an instant, jealousy swept through her. How had he known about this private little parlor? How many other women had he brought here? How many females had he pleasured in the same way, in nooks and alcoves and conveniently-empty music rooms?

It wasn't natural for a man to be so focused on his lover's pleasure that he didn't insist on his own – was it? How could he have maintained such a steady, steely presence of mind? Was the way he had touched her merely a mechanical process to him, something he had done so often that he could maintain perfect control of his own faculties while driving his partner mad?

As though he had heard her thoughts, James took her hand and slid it inside his coat, under the edge of his waistcoat, until her palm lay against the rapid, unsteady beat of his heart. "See what you do to me, Julia?"

They stood together that way for a long moment, their hands cupped together. Then without another word she left him there and went to join the ladies in the drawing room, her own heart still fluttering with the aftermath of his lovemaking.

She hoped to mingle around the edges of the crowd for a while, so no one would know for certain that she'd even been absent, but the instant she came into the drawing room, her friend Lady Hollowell spotted her. "Here's Julia now. You seem to have been missing forever, my dear. Are you unwell? You look flushed – I do hope you're not coming down with a fever, for I should hate for you to miss our outing to the opera."

The elderly, hawk-nosed Lady Stone spoke up. "Nonsense – I'm certain Julia is perfectly healthy." Her beady gaze focused on Julia's face, and her knowing smirk made her look like a wizened apple. "And, I gather, quite happy as well."

-5-

As they rode in the park a few days later, James said, "I understand you're attending the opera tonight."

Julia realized her thoughts had wandered back to the music room once more – prompted, she was reasonably certain, by the barest whiff of James's cologne and the sight of his strong hands on the reins of his roan. "Since when do you listen to the gossips?"

"Since I find them helpful in keeping track of your calendar. What is the performance to be?"

Julia bit her lip and dodged the question. "I can't think it matters a whit to you. I have it on the best authority that you detest opera and avoid it whenever possible."

"Oh, I do. I thought I might persuade you to change your plans."

"Certainly not," Julia said crisply. "Maria Hollowell is relying on me to help chaperone her younger sister."

He seemed amused at the idea of her as a chaperone, as well as undaunted by her refusal. "Very well, then. I must ask you, however…"

She almost held her breath.

"Why is it," he said gently, "that your sources are *the best authority* while mine are merely *gossips*?"

Julia released a long sigh and didn't bother to answer. She should have expected that he'd find some way to keep her off balance.

It was just as well he would not be at the opera. More distance from the overpowering experience in Lady Stone's music room would make her much more able to resist future temptation.

What distance? Here you are, riding with him in the park and listening to him talk nonsense – again!

But that was different, she argued. She *wasn't* riding with him, exactly; she was merely taking her regular outing. The fact that he'd drawn up beside her in the press of horses and riders was immaterial. Besides, if she had skipped her regular ride, after making such a fuss about how she tried never to miss an afternoon along Rotten Row, he'd have had reason to think she was going out of her way to avoid him. Which of course she wasn't; she was merely being cautious.

Her luck had almost run out entirely at Lady Stone's soiree. Fortunately, before Lady Hollowell had pressed Julia for an explanation, she'd been too distracted by her younger sister to fret any further about her friend. Clearly, however, Lady Stone had not been fooled for an instant.

What was it James had said about their hostess? *If she was not in the mood to wink at indiscretion, she'd have locked this room.* But even if that were true, Julia could not take the chance again. She just would not – *could* not – get caught up again in the sort of madness which had swept over her that night, even though the mere memory of that madness made her go all weak in the knees… to say nothing of sending a flood of embarrassing warmth to the most private parts of her body.

She shifted uncomfortably in her saddle and stole a glance at James, hoping he hadn't noticed how on edge she was. But she was not relieved when she realized he wasn't looking at her at all. Instead, he… was he actually eying one of this Season's debutantes?

He *was*, she thought in shock as the young woman – a beautiful blonde girl riding a big, showy black gelding – dimpled and smiled and ducked her head shyly as she and her friends approached. Julia glared at her, but the girl didn't seem to notice; she was casting sideways looks at James.

He tipped his hat to the group of young women, but he looked down at Julia. "Are you certain you won't reconsider the opera, my sweet?"

She wavered. What sort of entertainment did he intend to offer instead? There were so many to choose from these days – at least a dozen invitations for the evening lay on her desk at Sherwood House, many of which Julia would have preferred to attend. If Maria Hollowell hadn't insisted on the opera, Julia would be going to some ball or musicale or dinner party instead.

No doubt each of those locales offered a quiet little spot, suitable for seduction – and no doubt James knew them all.

Would that blonde young woman appear wherever he was going tonight, eager to draw his eye once more? With Julia safely tucked away at the opera, would he be tempted to flirt with the blonde, or to dance with her... or to do more?

Julia drew herself up with a shock. How utterly foolish she was being, to let a wave of jealousy get the better of her!

-6-

The opera was quite good, as operas went – but by the interval, Julia was doing her best not to yawn, and the only thing keeping her alert was her speculation about what James might be doing at the moment. She barely looked up as the door of Lady Hollowell's box opened, certain that the young gentleman who had begged the favor of bringing an ice for Lady Hollowell's sister had returned with the delicacy.

When she caught a whiff of familiar cologne, she turned her head so quickly her neck protested. "James!" She caught herself and looked around at the others in the box, but fortunately Maria Hollowell was too absorbed in her sister's budding romance to notice Julia's uncontrolled reaction. She added coolly, "I thought that you never go to the opera."

"As you so correctly observed, I avoid it whenever possible. However, when you are here, then it is not possible for me to avoid. *Res ipsa loquitur* – the thing speaks for itself."

Julia's heart skipped madly at the idea that he'd sacrificed whatever other entertainment had beckoned this evening, in order to be with her. But she wasn't about to let him see how delighted she was.

"Besides," he went on, "how could I pass by such an opportunity? When the company performs *The School for Lovers*, it simply begs for my attention." His eyes sparkled. "I must warn you, however, that I expect considerable favors in return. Come with me?"

"You wish to take a turn in the corridor before the next act?"

"Perhaps, though it would be better for your headache if you did not expose yourself to the rest of the music. Lady Hollowell, do not concern yourself about Lady Sherwood. I shall see her safely home."

Maria Hollowell's eyebrows nearly climbed into her hair, but before she could comment, James had draped Julia's cloak across his arm and swept her from the box.

He had already closed the door behind them before she pointed out, "I don't have a headache, James."

"I'm astounded, considering the volume of the music tonight – but also very glad, for in that case, I shall not take you *directly* home." He opened the door of the box next to Lady Hollowell's. The interior was in shadow, with only stray beams from the stage lighting briefly illuminating the curtains which were drawn all the way across the front.

Julia paused just inside to let her eyes adjust. "Whose box is this?"

"Ours – for tonight, at least." He turned the lock and advanced on her.

The sharp little click echoed against the murmur of conversation which oozed in through the thick curtains. Perhaps her hearing was heightened by the circumstances, but Julia was certain she could hear Lady Hollowell next door, giving her sister a soft-voiced scold. "You can't be serious. *Here*?"

"We'll simply be very quiet." James laughed at her expression. "You have no idea how adorable I find you, my sweet. You so clearly expect that my lovemaking will force you to scream your pleasure, no matter what's going on around you." He gathered her close as he spoke. "I find that assurance of yours very arousing."

The vibration of his voice against her temple, combined with the suggestive words, sent wetness surging between Julia's legs. She felt empty, achy, hollow – and oh, so eager.

As he kissed her long and slowly, she wondered for a moment what it was about James which could so quickly destroy her common sense and turn her resolution to naught. But the thought lasted only for a moment, because he perched her on the edge of a chair and knelt before her, gathering her skirt and petticoats around her waist and spreading her knees.

The first touch of his fingertips against her wet heat made her whimper, and when he flicked his tongue against her, she moaned. She barely noticed when the intermission was over and the orchestra once more began to play.

As he continued to slowly caress her with his mouth, sending waves of heat through her, Julia realized that the very effort to keep quiet actually increased the sensation. Every cry she held back made the pressure build, and every word she suppressed focused her pleasure more intensely. Finally she could bear no more, and she begged in a hoarse whisper for release. He held her firmly, darted his tongue once more, and she came apart in his arms. James gathered her close, cradling her and soothing her shudders. When she finally came back to herself, the box was filled with the ripple of music, the high notes of an aria seeming to echo from the walls and wrap around her as warmly as his arms. She was safe; she was comfortable; she was content to rest against him and, with her ear pressed to his chest, listen to his heartbeat.

Eventually she found her voice. "Did I scream?"

"Only a little." He kissed her ear and traced the lobe with the tip of his tongue. "You sounded more like the hiss of the final bit of steam escaping from a cooling kettle."

Julia glared at him. "It is not flattering to compare me to a teakettle!"

He laughed. "And your timing was exquisite as well. No one could have heard you over the screeching from the stage." He laid his cheek against her hair and held her tightly. "Julia, I am richly rewarded, and always surprised, by whatever you do. You are the most entertaining of mistresses."

Surely, Julia thought irritably, he hadn't stopped to think before speaking, or he wouldn't have made it sound as though he had myriads of women to compare her to. "I'm glad to find you so contented, sir, for that is the only reward you shall receive tonight."

He stopped the gentle exploration of her temple and paused for an instant, as if he'd heard the edge in her voice and was considering the reason. But when he spoke his voice was almost a purr. "Really? Do you mean that if I were to pick you up – so – and set you on my lap just like this…?"

She found herself straddling him with her skirts still hiked high, so that the only thing separating his heat and hers was the satin of his knee breeches – and she wasn't inclined to put too much faith in the strength of the fabric which barely contained his erection.

"Do you honestly believe that nothing more will happen?" he went on very softly.

Even in the dim light of the shadowed box, her eyes had adjusted enough to read the hunger in his gaze, and her reaction was shamefully rapid and so intense that she trembled against him.

"Stop squirming," he ordered, "or this will be very quick indeed."

Some part of her must have still been listening to the music, however, for suddenly she recognized the aria. "James," she gasped. "The last act is almost over. If we don't leave right now, then we'll likely encounter Lady Hollowell in the corridor, and we'll have to…." He nibbled at her breast, and she had to stop talking for a moment to get her breath. "To explain… why… we're still… here."

"I shall tell her how very persuasive you are. Or we could simply stay inside this box and enjoy each other until Lady Hollowell is long gone and the theater is empty. No one will come looking for us here."

Julia was so aroused that she actually considered the notion. "But we might get locked into the theater."

He gave a shout of laughter. "Oh, my Julia—"

"Yes, I know. I amuse you." Annoyed, she hopped off his lap before he could set her aside, and tripped over her hem. He caught her by her skirt, saving her a nasty – and probably loud – fall against the wall of the box, but the high waistline of her dress gave way under the pressure.

Julia looked down at her favorite evening gown, now not much more than a rag, and screeched in annoyance. What was wrong with her, anyway, to let him cozen her into behaving like a wanton?

James eyed the damage and said hopefully, "It could be worse."

"*How?*"

"You could have come out tonight without a wrap." He draped her black velvet cloak around her, and before she found her voice, he had swept her through the halls under the absent-minded gaze of those who had left the performance before the end in order to avoid the crush, and into a waiting carriage.

-7-

"My lady?" her maid said tentatively the following afternoon as she laid out a dress for Julia and arranged her hair in preparation for receiving callers.

Julia barely heard her, for she was bemoaning the fact that once more it was her regular afternoon at home to entertain her friends and callers. Though it was a warm, sunny, beautiful day, there would be no ride this afternoon – and therefore, no James, only a whole lot of very dull women munching on cakes and nattering on about everyone in the *ton*.

It was somewhat reassuring to know that as long as she was actually in the room, Julia herself wouldn't be the subject of gossip. Besides, listening to a couple of hours of that sort of discussion might serve to remind her to be more careful of her own reputation – which she certainly had not been at the opera.

How easily James had drawn her into making love with him! It had been sheerest chance that she'd recognized the final aria and realized how much time had passed. Of course, they *could* have waited for the entire crowd to clear – though how would they have known when it was safe to come out? And if they had waited too long, and been locked in together for the night…

James would have managed to keep me entertained.

She felt herself coloring as she thought about all the things he might have done, given complete privacy and the entire night. With an effort, she dismissed that daydream. She could hardly have trailed back to Bruton Street barely in time for breakfast, when the opera had been over for hours.

No, she simply must be more careful. At the Spragues' upcoming ball, she would not allow James to lure her away from the crowd. She had an advantage this time; she would not be surprised when he turned up, for he'd told her he was coming. And he'd whispered something about an alcove under the stairs at the Spragues' house – so she knew exactly in which direction danger lay. *Stay away from the stairways,* she reminded herself, *and you'll be just fine.*

Belatedly, she realized she hadn't answered her maid. "Yes, Mary? What is it?"

"Your blue gown, ma'am – the one you wore to the opera last night. I thought at first the seams had simply come unstitched and I could fix the damage, but as you can see, the fabric tore right down the skirt."

Julia sighed. "I know. I was there. I don't suppose there's enough extra width in the skirt to take that section out?"

"It would make a very awkward seam, ma'am."

"I was afraid of that. Well, put it aside for now. Perhaps next year, round gowns will be out of fashion once more and we can make a virtue of that gash up the front."

While she finished coiling her mistress's glossy dark hair, Mary looked at her as if she feared Julia had lost her reason. "I just don't understand how stepping on your hem while you climbed the steps at the opera house could have caused all that damage, ma'am."

"Never mind, Mary. These things happen." Julia gave herself a cursory glance in the mirror. "Very nice," she murmured as she stood up to have her gown laced up the back.

She had dawdled till the last possible moment, and she had barely reached the drawing room and taken her place in her favorite chair when the butler announced her first callers. "Lady Hollowell, ma'am, and Lady Stone."

Julia smothered a sigh and stood to receive the ladies. "What a delight to see you again, Lady Stone." She curtseyed. "And Maria – I must beg your pardon for abandoning you last night."

Lady Hollowell advanced on her. "For someone who suffered from headache last night, you look remarkably well today, Julia."

"I had no idea you were subject to headache," Lady Stone sympathized. "What a dreadful affliction, but obviously you found a treatment which relieved your discomfort tolerably well."

"I have always found it most helpful to rest in a darkened room," Julia said. She wasn't lying, she told herself, only failing to correct a mistaken impression. Besides, the box at the opera *had* been dark. Before the ladies could begin comparing notes on various treatments, she went straight on. "Tea will be here in a moment, I believe."

"I never drink the stuff," Lady Stone said. "We ran into Sherwood in the hall as we came in, and I asked him for a glass of port instead."

Julia's insides went shivery. Her husband was actually here in the house, in the middle of the afternoon? Normally he'd have left hours ago. What had made him change his routine, and why hadn't she had so much as a hint of his presence? But startled as she was, she had to repress a giggle at the idea of Lord Sherwood taking orders from Lady Stone as though he were a servant in his own house.

Lady Stone went on comfortably, "Even your over-starched butler can't object to my tastes under those circumstances."

What circumstances? Before Julia could ask, the drawing room door opened and her husband came in, followed by a footman bringing tea and the butler himself bearing a silver tray of wineglasses and decanters.

Lady Stone patted the settee beside her in invitation. "I hoped you'd be along shortly, Sherwood," she cackled. "It's much more fun to drink port with the master of the house than in solitary state."

Lord Sherwood bowed to Lady Stone and Lady Hollowell, and then came to bend over Julia's hand. Despite her best efforts to behave naturally, she stiffened. He must have noticed her reaction, she thought, for his gaze sharpened. "You seemed shocked to see me, my dear."

"You never come to my at-homes." She settled herself behind the tea tray and began to pour.

"How thoughtless I have been," he said mildly. "I felt it was time to repair the lack."

"That only means there's nothing of importance happening in the Lords today," Lady Stone said shrewdly. "Or are you checking to see what your wife has been getting up to these days while you're playing your political games?"

"I have no doubt she is keeping herself well-entertained while I deal with matters of state," Sherwood said. "My wife is both capable and efficient."

What perfectly tepid praise, Julia thought.

Sherwood had gone on as though the subject of Julia no longer interested him. "Did you enjoy the opera last night, Lady Hollowell?"

"I always appreciate *The School for Lovers*, my lord – though not as much as if Julia had felt well enough to stay for the entire performance. Such a pity, the headache she suffered."

"Indeed? What a pity – though you seem to have promptly recovered from the affliction, my dear." Lord Sherwood poured a glass of port for Lady Stone. "*The School for Lovers*? I hope the performance is not as risqué as it sounds, lest it serve as an instructional manual for London's ladies."

"Oh, no one goes to the opera for the subject matter," Lady Stone said comfortably. "Only to see and be seen. Or – occasionally – to *not* be seen, when one is up to no good."

Julia wondered uneasily if that was merely an idle comment or if the old lady was sending a meaningful look – or perhaps even a warning – in her direction.

"Come and tell me about Barton's speech in the Lords yesterday, Sherwood," Lady Stone commanded. "And by the by, this is very good port."

Sherwood stayed for the absolutely proper twenty minutes, greeting each of the additional ladies who came to call. The drawing room was crowded by the time he left, murmuring something about a debate which was scheduled to start soon.

The moment he was out of sight, Lady Carruthers came to sit beside Julia. "How very odd of your husband to intrude on your visiting hours."

Julia could almost see Lady Carruthers sorting through possibilities and circling in on the most titillating of them, and she spoke quickly to try to deflect the woman's curiosity. "I believe he came only to put Lady Stone at ease."

Lady Carruthers looked at her with something very like pity. "You can't truly think that, since Lady Stone hasn't been ill at ease in the fifty years since she left her governess's side." She let her voice drop to a scandalized whisper. "What's really going on, Julia? Do you think Sherwood could be... well... spying on you? What have you been up to, that you've aroused his suspicions?"

-8-

Stay away from the stairway, Julia reminded herself as she arrived at the Spragues' house in Cavendish Square. Except that of course she couldn't avoid it entirely, for the ladies' withdrawing room was at the top of the main stair. She left her cloak with the maid there and joined a group of ladies on their way to the ballroom at the back of the main floor, where a row of doors led onto a terrace which overlooked the elaborate garden.

She couldn't help but eye the base of the staircase as she passed, and she wondered what on earth James had been talking about. There seemed no place which could possibly be secret enough to snatch a kiss, much less anything more. Perhaps he'd confused the house with another of the mansions on Cavendish Square. The man seemed to have catalogued the secret nooks and crannies of every dwelling in Mayfair. With so many to keep straight, Julia supposed it should be no surprise if he sometimes couldn't keep them straight.

She wondered if he could remember which ladies he'd accompanied to each of those secret spots, as well as which places – and which ladies – were his favorites. And then she told herself that jealousy was a foolish emotion when one was carrying on an affair.

She was fashionably late, and the ball had already begun as she greeted her hostess, exclaimed over the daughter of the house in whose honor the affair was being given, and collected her dance card.

James appeared only a few minutes later, something Julia knew instantly because of the way her senses piqued. How foolish, she told herself, to be so aware of him that in the midst of a crowd her skin would begin to prickle the moment he walked into a room.

He saw her right away too, she was certain – though it took him some time to cross the room as he stopped to greet at least a dozen people along the way. How careful he was not to draw the attention of the gossips by striking out straight toward her. Unless, of course, it happened to suit him to get the *ton* talking.

She wondered uneasily where that thought had come from. Surely James would never decide that stirring up gossip would be amusing – though she had to admit he had a quirky sense of humor.

"Were you waiting for me?" he asked softly as he came up beside her.

"You mean because I am not dancing? Alas, I could not make up my mind who to favor among the half-dozen gentlemen who asked for my hand. I delayed too long in choosing, so here I stand forlorn while they are all off wooing other ladies."

"That is the peril of indecision," James agreed. He took her dance card and inspected its barren lines. "Or, possibly, of being so late to arrive that the first set has already begun."

Julia gave a theatrical sigh. "Must you always puncture my self-importance?"

He slashed his name across her card and handed it back. "Until the first waltz, my sweet. I shall be waiting impatiently."

He gave no evidence of impatience, however, as he moved off to talk to a couple of gentlemen standing at the door of a room set aside for cards.

When the orchestra struck up the first waltz, she didn't need to look around for him; she knew the instant he started toward her. He swept her out onto the well-polished floor, and to her surprise he didn't even move them toward the corner of the room, much less maneuver her out of the ballroom. "I see you realize your error," she said as they made their third circle of the floor.

James looked puzzled. "Error?"

"About the stairway. There's no alcove under the stairway in this house. It's entirely open. Were you thinking of some other family named Sprague, perhaps?"

He grinned. "Have you spent all this time dreaming about a tryst under the stairs, my sweet?"

She almost stumbled, and he drew her closer to steady her steps. How foolish of her to admit she remembered what he'd said days ago about the Sprague house, much less confess that she'd actually been intrigued enough to go looking.

"What an eager little lover you are," he murmured. "The entire point of a private alcove is that it's not easily visible to passersby. There also happens to be more than one staircase in this house. Shall I show you the one I was referring to?"

Heat washed over her at the sultry suggestion. "It isn't fair, you know – what you do to me. And in *public*."

"Then let us be private. I have a friend who owns a house just off Portman Square. Can you get away next Wednesday afternoon?"

She frowned. "You wish to take me to visit a friend?"

"Oh, no. He doesn't actually live there – and he'll loan me the key, I am certain."

Julia was aghast. "You cannot be serious! You want me to join you in – in your friend's love nest?"

"It's not so much a love nest as it is a house for unconventional people."

"I don't want to ask what that means. Do I know this gentleman's wife?"

"Without a doubt. In case it's a comfort to you, I can assure you that the wife in question knows all about it."

"Just because a wife recognizes the reality of her husband's activities doesn't mean she wants all her friends to know about his mistresses, or to visit the place!"

He looked down at her thoughtfully. "I assure you there's nothing at all off-color. It's quite an ordinary little house, really, so if you're expecting some sort of bordello..."

Julia gave him the haughtiest look she could muster. "I wish to hear no more about it. In any case, I am to drive in the park on Wednesday afternoon, with Lady Hollowell and Lady Carruthers."

"That's a pity. But perhaps there will be another time."

Had he not heard her? Could she possibly have made herself any clearer on the subject?

But Julia realized to her embarrassment that it wasn't only indignation she was feeling, but regret. The very idea of spending an entire afternoon with James, in a completely private, secret little spot… There were so few places where such a thing was even possible, and the opportunity might never come again.

But what a fool she was even to let herself consider going with him to a private home – a little house which even James admitted had been deliberately set up by a gentleman to house a mistress. What was she *thinking*?

-9-

On the Wednesday which he had suggested for a private tryst, Julia kept her promise and went driving in the park – where she was bored out of her mind by the inane chatter of Lady Hollowell and Lady Carruthers as they commented on the weather and speculated on the matches which had already been announced and those which seemed likely to be upcoming in the *ton*.

Midway through their drive, Julia realized she was watching the crowd and hoping to catch a glimpse of James. Not that he would be in the park today, of course, since he knew she wasn't riding.

But she couldn't help wondering where he might be instead. Of course it was downright foolish of her to speculate – even for a moment – whether he might have found someone else to keep him company in that hidden-away little house just off Portman Square. James wasn't like that, she told herself, even if his friend was.

How close a friend did a gentleman have to be, anyway, to loan out his love nest?

For once, she almost missed James in the crowd – mostly because she had convinced herself that he could not possibly be there. When she spotted him across the park on his roan gelding, she had to look twice to convince herself she hadn't imagined him there – but then she went all lax and liquid with relief.

"What is the matter with you today, Julia?" Maria Hollowell said almost crossly. "That's the second time you've said something that makes no sense at all. Are you so fearfully distracted? I thought you were having such a good time this year!"

Indeed she had been having a wonderful Season – all because of James, of course. But her friends would be shocked if she admitted it, so Julia changed the subject. "I just have other things on my mind, I suppose. I received a letter from Everleigh this morning, from my baby's nurse."

Lady Carruthers gasped. "He's not ill, is he?"

"Oh, no – but he seems to be growing so fast, and I'm missing it all."

Maria shook her head. "Julia, dear, you hired the best baby nurse to be found, and I know for a fact what you're paying her because I would have hired her away from you if I could afford to. For that kind of money, she no doubt counts his every breath. She'll take far better care of him than you could."

"Take my advice," Lady Carruthers chimed in, "and don't say a word to Sherwood in case he thinks you actually want to go home. No husband enjoys the Season, you know, so he might seize the opportunity to sweep you off to rusticate."

"Not Sherwood," Maria chimed in. "He's too absorbed in his politics to leave London as long as the Lords are in session."

"In that case, he might even send Julia home and stay himself," Lady Carruthers mused. "Do be careful not to give him an excuse – and I don't mean just this longing for your son. He already seems to be keeping a careful eye on you, so don't be a nodcock. Enjoy yourself whenever Sherwood's back is turned, for the Season will be over soon enough."

Maria chimed in, "I heard just this morning that the Ilfords have already gone back to Yorkshire. Why they'd be in a hurry to return there, of all places...."

-10-

The Season will be over soon enough. The refrain seemed to echo through Julia's head, and as she was dressing for a card party she paused to count on her calendar, startled to realize that Lady Carruthers had been right.

Julia had barely noticed the weeks slipping away. She had been so caught up in riding with James, or dancing with James, or flirting with James – or, failing all of those pastimes, simply thinking about James – that she hadn't paid attention. Now she realized that far less remained of the Season than had already passed.

She watched from the carriage window as she was driven to the party. Was it her imagination, or was more of Mayfair dark tonight than usual? And did that lack of light in the windows she passed mean that the owners of those houses were, like Julia, going out for the evening, or that they'd already packed up and gone home – wherever home might be?

The sense that her special time was drawing to a close made her jittery. Though she had never exactly been good at cards, she was generally a competent player – but tonight she couldn't concentrate at all.

Eventually Lady Stone, who was not the hostess but who dominated any card party she attended, ordered Julia away from the table. "Go get a breath of fresh air before you manage to lose your husband's entire holdings," she snapped. "I'll do better with no partner at all!" She turned immediately back to sorting her hand.

With relief, Julia stepped out onto a wide terrace overlooking the Thames. Though the calendar hadn't lied, the soft spring air confirmed for her how much time had passed. Just weeks ago – when her affair with James had started – it would have been too cold to stand here in a thin dinner dress and no cloak.

She didn't turn when she heard his soft footsteps on the flagstones, but she shivered in eagerness.

"Shall I help you stay warm?" James whispered into her ear.

"Are you offering me your coat, sir?"

"Of course not." He drew her into his arms instead and bent his head to kiss her.

She gave a squeak of surprise and glanced toward the card tables, only a few feet away inside the brilliantly-lit drawing room.

"Card players never notice anything outside the bounds of the table." He kissed her long and slowly and then leaned back, his hands clasped on her waist, to study her face. "What's wrong, my sweet? You taste desperate, somehow. Do you still regret missing our tryst so you could go driving in the park?"

"Of course not." She spoke too quickly, and his dubious look made her stammer. "Well... perhaps."

"A pity, of course, for it was a splendid idea – but it's just as well that you turned down my invitation."

"It is?" She frowned.

"I spoke without thinking. As it turns out, my friend had made plans, so it would not have been possible to borrow the house after all."

She had to admit to a trickle of disappointment.

Clearly James could read what she was thinking. "If you will join me the day after tomorrow, I'll see what I can do."

He kissed her again before she could answer, and by the time he was finished, Julia's resolution – and, she feared, any morals she still possessed – had melted away. "Yes," she whispered, and he rewarded her with another of the beautiful smiles which always left her sizzling with longing.

-11-

On the appointed afternoon, Julia walked toward Bond Street and climbed into a hackney carriage which idled along the road waiting for her, just as James's note had promised.

With every street they passed, her heart pounded faster. She hadn't quite realized until she'd embarked on this adventure that it was dangerous to come alone to heaven knows where. She was putting herself into the hands of people she didn't know and had no reason to trust.

Oh, not James, of course; she could rely on him. But she didn't even know where she was going, and for that matter, neither did anyone else. If she simply vanished, no one would have any idea where to look for her.

The little house near Portman Square, she supposed. James's seductive kisses had clouded her mind, or she would have renewed her objections. Borrowing a love nest from a gentleman was very much the same as approving that gentleman's pursuits, and that was something Julia simply could not do. A gentleman's wife had few enough rights and privileges; she could not control her husband's actions, but at the least she deserved the respect of every other gentleman's wife.

But no, Julia realized – the hackney was heading in another direction entirely. She was glad that at least James had taken her concerns seriously, even though she was at a complete loss to know where he might be meeting her.

A few minutes later, the hackney drew up in front of the Red Dragon coaching inn on the Islington Road. A post-chaise stood in front with a team already in place, and another had just swept into the yard where the ostlers swarmed around to unhitch the horses and lead them away.

A coaching inn? Surely James wasn't foolish enough to think she was going to run away with him. She almost ordered the hackney driver to take her straight back to Bruton Street, but in truth she was so jittery after the ride that she just wanted out of that small, cramped carriage. Surely she could hire some sort of conveyance here to get her home – couldn't she?

She drew down the dark veil attached to her hat and waited for the hackney driver to open the door and help her down. Instead, the scent of James's cologne tickled her nose as he effortlessly lifted her from the carriage. Relief surged through her, but rather than admit how pleased she was to see him, Julia looked around and wrinkled her nose. "It's a bit busy here, don't you think?"

"You were hoping for something more private? Sometimes a more crowded spot makes it easier to be alone." James slapped his hand against the side of the hackney. The driver touched his whip to his hat brim, and the carriage pulled into the road and headed back toward the center of the city.

James offered his arm. "Shall we go in? My friend's house was not available today, either, but I thought this a passable substitute."

"Why? Is he using his little love nest himself?" Julia reminded herself that she was hardly in any position to cast stones – though at least James wasn't cheating on a wife. Gentlemen did this sort of thing, and her getting irate about it wouldn't change the facts.

"Shame, isn't it?" James's tone was droll. "Just because he owns the place, he believes he has first claim on using it."

Off to the right by the main door was a taproom, noisy and busy even at this hour of the afternoon. To the left was a short hallway containing a row of doors – private parlors reserved for the use of travelers for meals or as they waited for fresh horses. But James led her straight ahead, to a steep staircase.

The room he took her to must have been the best in the inn, large and airy. It might, she thought, have originally been two rooms, because there was a fireplace at each end. One side of the room was set up as a sort of parlor with a table and a couple of chairs set near the crackling fire, while the other end...

At the sight of the big bed with its bright pieced and quilted coverlet, she hesitated – and then laughed at herself for being so missish over such an ordinary piece of furniture, after the things they had done together all spring. She took off her hat and went to inspect the tray which waited on the table. Tea, steam wafting comfortably from the spout of the pot. Strawberries and cream, and scones, and small cakes. And champagne. "I see there is nothing left to chance," she murmured, and turned her back to him. "If you'll unlace me, please?"

"You do not want tea first?" But he was nuzzling her nape, and the rush of heat which swept through her burned away any desire for food or drink.

Her voice was lower than usual, and raspy. "I can have tea anytime."

She thought his fingertips trembled a bit as he undressed her and tucked her very gently under the quilted coverlet and joined her there.

The tea grew cold on the table while they explored each other, free at last to take their time. She did not need to fret about tell-tale wrinkles in her skirts, since her dress lay neatly over one of the chairs by the fire rather than being hiked up around her as it had been in the box at the opera. He need not exercise caution about her elegant coiffure, as he had on nearly every other occasion when he had kissed her, since today she had coiled her hair up under her hat in a casual style she could reproduce without the help of her maid. And though she was still mildly aware of the possibility of being overheard by some passerby in the corridor, the anonymity and privacy of the inn – along with the sheer magic of his kisses, his whispers, his caresses – washed away any hesitation she felt.

Their lovemaking was slow and gentle. In their sometimes-hurried, always risky encounters, Julia had not felt truly free to search and scrutinize and experiment. Throughout the Season, he had made love to her in ways she had never imagined, but in the bedroom of the Red Dragon, she could make love to him. She discovered an entirely new level of fulfillment and joy when at last she could satisfy him, and she realized with humble awe the power that she had over this man that she had fallen in love with.

In turn, James explored her body as thoroughly as if he'd never had the freedom to touch her before but now had all the time in the world – and when she gave herself fully to him, she felt such intense satisfaction as he possessed her that she thought there could be no greater joy in the world.

Afterward, they lay together, spent and satiated, until he rose and brought back champagne and strawberries and cakes so they could picnic in their bed. He fed her, and she fed him, and then he drizzled champagne over her and slowly licked it off her skin, nibbling gently until she climaxed just from his touch. When she finally stopped trembling, she smiled up at him – and was startled into immobility by the fierce, hungry gleam in his eyes and the firmness of his hands as he arranged her body to suit himself and took her once more, not at all gently – and yet with such intensity for them both that she shrieked when he finally allowed her release.

-12-

But now, just a few days after the long and luxurious afternoon they had spent at the Red Dragon, Julia had received a message at the breakfast table setting an assignation in Bond Street, outside her milliner's shop… and Lord Sherwood had announced his plans to return home to Everleigh no later than the end of the week.

Perhaps it was just as well that their affair was coming to an end, Julia thought. They couldn't keep on this way, maintaining this peak of emotional involvement, of excitement, of thrill-seeking danger. They couldn't continue taking the chance that they'd be discovered somewhere, in an alcove or under a set of stairs – and after the satisfaction of a private parlor at the Red Dragon, she suspected that a surreptitious kiss would be no more satisfying than a tepid cup of tea.

Their affair had no future. Melancholy tugged at Julia as she climbed into the carriage which the coachman brought to the front door of the house in Bruton Street, and as they picked their way through Mayfair to the milliner's shop.

If she had needed evidence that the Season was coming to an end, she could have found it in Bond Street, where the traffic was no longer a constant crush and the tradesmen were not so frantically busy as they had been earlier in the year. Here and there ladies were shopping for trousseaus, or for upcoming trips to Bath or Brighton, or for the last few things they might need at their summer homes.

Outside your milliner's shop, James had written – but he was not there, so Julia went inside.

The milliner herself was waiting on a couple of customers – one of the Season's debutantes and her mother, who were arguing over which style of hat would be suitable for the girl's wedding.

Since she was in no hurry, Julia set her hatbox down and dawdled around the showroom, keeping a careful eye on the front window. She didn't need another riding bonnet, though the one on display atop a pedestal in a prominent corner would be fiercely becoming – more so, in fact, than the one she'd brought back for repair. She looked it over closely, wondering what James would say if she turned up in the park wearing the audacious bonnet.

But she turned away from it with a sigh. She didn't need such a thing at home at Everleigh, and she had already exceeded her budget for clothing and what Sherwood called fripperies.

Finally the hat-buying customers departed with no decision made, and the milliner turned her attention to Julia, exclaiming when she saw the loose trim on the edge of the new hat. Her nimble fingers made short work of the repair.

Julia gathered up her hatbox and went out. The time was a couple of minutes after eleven, but there was still no sign of James.

With her business done, she had no excuse to linger outside the shop. She walked as slowly as she could down Bond Street, pretending to study merchandise in each window she passed, in no hurry to catch up with the carriage she had sent to wait for her at the far end of the street.

Perhaps James had been detained by some legitimate business, something which had arisen after he had penned that note and sent it off to her. It really was quite unusual that something of the sort hadn't happened before, in all these weeks they'd been meeting.

Or perhaps he no longer found the intrigue of their affair as entertaining as he had at the beginning. Had she turned out to be a disappointment to him? Once he had won her, was she no longer an exciting conquest?

She told herself that her gloomy feeling was merely her own fears talking, but she couldn't quite shake the sense that the entire thing had been nothing more than a game to James – and perhaps a game he had played before. The adventure and the intrigue and the danger were all new to her – but had he found himself becoming bored by what might, to him, be nothing so exciting after all? Had he grown weary of her hesitation, of her concern for what others might think?

While their tryst at the Red Dragon had been intense and unique and wonderful, that had been days ago, and there hadn't been another note until this morning. Had their afternoon of lovemaking been his chief goal all along, and once it was achieved he no longer felt the same level of desire for her?

Perhaps it was time to go home, she thought. Back to Everleigh, and her son, and her duties as Lord Sherwood's wife.

She wandered past a jeweler's shop and paused to glance at a necklace in the window, just as James opened the door and stepped out onto the street.

All her common-sense scolding seemed to evaporate in a sudden rush of gladness. He hadn't abandoned her; he hadn't found some other pastime more inviting.

"Don't you know the difference between jewelry and hats?" she said, sounding far calmer than she felt. "What were you thinking, anyway, to suggest meeting on Bond Street? It's hardly a secret spot for an assignation."

He smiled and took her hat box out of her hands. "Enjoyable as a completely private afternoon can be, you must admit there's something thrilling about meeting a lover in a place like this."

"Where someone might notice at any moment, you mean."

"Exactly." He drew her into the shadow of the bay window at the corner of the jeweler's shop. "I must apologize for my lateness, my sweet. I was delayed."

She said carelessly, "I suppose buying a new watch fob is more important than our meeting."

"Of course it is. A gentleman can always use a new watch fob." He drew a slim black leather case from his coat. "Would you care to see it?"

"I am not generally considered an authority on watch fobs."

"Good. Then you will not criticize my taste." He snapped the box open.

Even in the shadow cast by the storefront and the bay window, light caught and sparkled off the long row of brilliant white stones which formed the most beautiful diamond bracelet Julia had ever seen. She couldn't help but draw in a long breath of astonishment.

"Oh, dear," James said. "The jeweler seems to have made a terrible mistake. This isn't a watch fob after all. Whatever will I do with a lady's bracelet?"

"I'm certain you'll think of something." Julia's tone was dry.

The humor died out of James's eyes. "What's wrong?"

She bit her lip hard, and said finally, "Gentlemen give such things to their mistresses when they wish to be rid of them."

"I can't speak for other gentlemen, but I give such things when I wish a very special lady to remember me with fondness."

Oh, I'll remember you. No gifts required. She sighed. "Lady Stone's ball is only a few days off, and then the Season will begin to wind down."

"Nothing lasts forever," he pointed out gently. "Wear this to the ball, for me?"

Sadness trickled through Julia's veins. He couldn't have made it any more apparent that their affair was indeed coming to a close. They would make love for the last time in the same place where they had begun, and she would go home with a diamond bracelet, and memories…

"Save me all the waltzes," James said.

"*All* of them? What a feast that will make for the gossips!"

James leaned closer, until his whisper stirred the tendrils of hair beside her ear. "Not if we don't waste precious time dancing."

-13-

Lady Stone's house in Grosvenor Square was even more brilliantly lit – and far more crowded – than it had been at her soiree earlier in the Season. It would be a wonder if James could even find her in the crush, Julia thought as she wriggled through the throng of people at the edge of the ballroom.

Though she had arrived in plenty of time for the start of the dancing, she hadn't yet laid eyes on James. He'd even missed the first waltz, which she'd spent tapping her toe at the edge of the ballroom. She would have been annoyed with him, if she hadn't been so determined not to ruin their very last evening together with petty concerns. He must have been delayed again, that was all. He would come.

Nearby, she heard Maria Hollowell quietly scolding her sister for conduct unbecoming a debutante. After the chastened girl went back out on the floor for the next country dance, Maria came to stand beside Julia with a sigh. "This business of looking out for a debutante is far more of a nuisance than I expected. What trials we must have been to our chaperones. Why aren't you dancing tonight?"

"Sore toe," Julia said lightly. "Someone stepped on it as I came into the ballroom."

"Pity. Too bad you can't find a chair in this crush, to rest your foot."

"An excellent notion. Perhaps I'll go up to the cloakroom."

"I'd go along, if I didn't have to keep such a close eye on my sister."

That fact was precisely what Julia had counted on. She turned away with a smile to survey the crowd, and her gaze fell on Lord Sherwood at the very moment he bowed before them. "Lady Hollowell, it's a pleasure to see you here. Julia, what a lovely bracelet you're wearing tonight." He reached for her hand, holding it up to inspect the bracelet, clasped around her wrist over her glove, as it gleamed in the candlelight.

"Isn't it just?" Lady Hollowell murmured. "But do you mean you didn't buy it for her, my lord? I wish I had enough pin money to buy things like that."

"Pin money?" Lord Sherwood lifted one eyebrow. "I had no idea I was being so generous with your allowance, my dear. We really must discuss the matter sometime."

Julia sucked in a breath just as her partner for the next country dance appeared. Relieved of the need to answer, she tucked her hand into her partner's arm and turned toward the newly-forming set just as Maria Hollowell said, "Lord Sherwood, I do hope I can persuade you to find room in your evening to share a country dance with my sister."

"Perhaps she has this one available," he said agreeably.

Julia found herself just a few places down the set from Lord Sherwood and Maria Hollowell's sister, and several times as the dance proceeded and they passed by each other, she felt his gaze resting on the bracelet. "Pin money," he said once, sounding doubtful, in a moment when they were close enough to speak.

There was far too much of a crush to enjoy dancing, especially when she'd rather be somewhere else. After the country dance ended, Julia spent nearly ten minutes working her way along the perimeter of the ballroom, feeling more impatient with every second and more eager to get to the music room, where surely James would join her soon.

This was their last evening together. It would be the last kiss of their affair. The last caress. The last… well, whatever James had in mind for tonight. She felt color creep into her cheeks at the thought of what he might do, given even a few delicious minutes together in that quiet room.

She was startled to find the hallway outside the ballroom empty. Everyone who was coming to the ball had arrived; everyone who was sitting out a dance in the refreshment room had gone downstairs; everyone who had retreated to the cloakroom to rest or fix a mishap with a dress had climbed out of sight. How perfectly convenient.

She walked past the music room door, suddenly feeling a bit shy about going in by herself. Instead she dawdled for a moment in the shadow of an alcove, making certain she was unobserved, before strolling back toward her destination – hoping that James would come. She looked up with anticipation when the ballroom doors opened, but it wasn't James. Instead, a young man and a matron came out of the ballroom, and Julia paused, pretending to admire a painting of some long-dead ancestor of the Stone family, as she waited for them to go out of sight. But they didn't; a moment later Lady Stone caught up with them, and right after her, another couple appeared, walking toward the stairs…

Oh, *why* hadn't she ducked into the music room right away? Now she'd have to wait until this crowd went away.

James came up behind her just as Lady Stone flung open the music room door to reveal a young couple with their clothes in disarray. Chaos broke out as everyone in the hall began to chatter about the scandalous sight.

Another few minutes, and that could have been us. Julia's heart was pounding so loudly she was amazed that no one in the hall was looking at her. But then, at least she still had all her clothes on.

"That delay was good timing on your part," James said calmly. "Isn't that Lady Stone's companion? One would think since she has the use of the house all the time, she could leave the music room for guests on special occasions like a ball."

Try as she might, Julia could detect nothing but good humor in his voice. But that was James, she thought – always in control. As for her…

She felt cheated, and angry, and frustrated, and miserable at losing these last few precious moments.

She had so counted on just one last time, one last memory.

But also, she had to admit, she'd been shocked back to her senses. It was past time for her to go home.

-14-

The carriage bearing the Sherwood crest drew away from the London house in good time, though admittedly not quite as early as Lord Sherwood had wished. It would be followed in good time by a second coach carrying the baggage, watched over by his lordship's valet and her ladyship's maid. Julia watched from the carriage window as they drove from Mayfair through the city, storing up the noises and the smells and the hullaballoo to keep in her memory until next year.

Finally, when the countryside began to unroll before them, quiet and green and peaceful with villages sprinkled here and there, she settled back into her seat and looked across at her husband.

Lord Sherwood had unfolded a letter on his knee and seemed to be giving the communication his full attention. He seemed to feel her gaze on him, however, for he looked up quizzically. "What is it, ma'am?"

She took a deep breath. "Must I wait until next Season to see him again?"

"Who? Your lover, the London dandy? I think you'd be well-advised to leave him in the city. He wouldn't fit at all well at a country estate."

"Not even at the odd house party?" Her tone was wistful.

"Perhaps," he conceded. "Though if you expect to be as bored at Everleigh as you were in London, the occasional house party will doubtless not be enough to keep you entertained."

"I shall not be bored, exactly, for there is plenty to do. But..."

"But you expect to miss him."

She nodded.

He picked up his letter again. "I believe there's a country squire in the neighborhood who is every bit as mad for you as your London swain is."

She perked up. "Really?"

"I expect he would be agreeable to showing you the pleasures of long rides in the country, and picnics in the woods, and perhaps even moonlight swims in the lake."

"Oh. In that case, I probably shan't miss my London lover at all." She bounced in her seat and noted the intense way her husband was looking at her. "Though I suppose you think I shouldn't say so, since it might hurt his feelings."

He laughed. "You are an incorrigible flirt, Julia."

Suddenly serious, she said, "Is that why you did it? Because you thought I'd be tempted to flirt with some other gentleman, so you wanted to keep me too busy to look around for a lover?"

"No, because I trust you, as well as being madly in love with you. But you must admit that you enjoyed the risk and the thrill and the excitement and the danger of your London affair – even if your illicit lover was also your staid husband."

"Never *staid*. Not you, James."

"Admit it, my dear. You thought that once married and settled down, I was growing positively stodgy."

"Perhaps at first," she admitted. "Not after Lady Stone's soiree." She blushed, remembering. "At any rate, it was fun. All of it."

"And it will be again, next Season. In the meantime…"

"Did you say long rides?" *Perhaps I should have bought that outrageous bonnet after all.* "And picnics? And moonlight swims?" A thrill of anticipation ran through her at the idea of what he might do in that sort of surroundings. "I can't wait to get home to Everleigh."

"Don't be in too much of a rush," James said. "I haven't yet shared with you the reason why a long journey in a closed carriage is not something to dread. But we have all day, if you'd like me to demonstrate." He didn't wait for an answer but reached up to release the curtains, to shut away the world.

In the sudden dimness of the carriage he moved across to sit beside her, one arm around her and the other hand cupping her chin, holding her face at just the right angle for his kiss. The scent of his cologne swirled around and through her, as intoxicating as it had been on the night he had proposed their affair.

She kissed him with everything he had taught her through this Season, her mouth open and hot and demanding, and he responded by pulling her onto his lap.

"Yes, please," Julia said demurely. "Demonstrate."

"And I believe we were going to discuss the matter of pin money as well," he whispered in her ear. "Did you lie to Maria Hollowell about how you got that bracelet?"

"Oh, shush." Julia wriggled, enjoying the sensation of him hardening under her, until she'd turned enough to cup his face in her hands. She kissed him long and slowly before moving on to even more interesting pursuits.

And when some hours later the carriage reached Everleigh, it was a thoroughly disheveled and contented Lady Sherwood who allowed her husband – her lover – to lift her down and carry her into their home.

Wedding Daze

Emily let her gaze drift across the ballroom, only half-hearing the voice of the girl standing next to her. "When is the wedding?" Annabelle asked, and Emily wanted to say, "*Never*."

But of course there would be a wedding. The agreements had all been made, the marriage contracts had been signed, the announcements had been published, and the banns had been read. So the wedding would happen as scheduled, on Saturday, in the private chapel of the Marquess of Bristol's London house – because once things had reached the stage of agreements, contracts, announcements and banns, there could be no other course of action. A bride who backed out of her wedding would be ruined indeed.

And that was no less true even when the bride in question suspected that her life would be just as much a ruin if she went through with the wedding.

"He's so gorgeous," Annabelle went on. "Harry, I mean. All the girls think so."

That was a good share of the problem, Emily thought as she looked across the ballroom once more to where Harry – Lord Henry Warrender, the second son of the Marquess of Bristol – was dancing with Cassandra Sprague. And the rest of the problem was that Harry – the man she was supposed to marry on Saturday – reciprocated that sentiment. He thought that the girls were gorgeous too. Every last one of them. Society miss or stage actress. Simpering debutante or worldly widow.

For Harry was a rake. There was simply no denying that – and in fact no one ever tried. Certainly Emily's father had not minced words, when he'd called Emily into his book room to tell her about the offer for her hand – which had been made not by Harry himself, he informed her, but by Harry's father, the Marquess of Bristol, over a hand of piquet and a glass of wine at their gentlemen's club.

*****

"Harry's been wild since his mother died," Sir Walter Moore had told her, in his gruff but not unloving manner. "Bristol thinks it'll settle him down – marrying him off to a sensible, steady girl like you."

"I'm honored, Father," Emily had said.

Sensible. Steady. Yes, she thought wryly, that was the exact description a young woman in her third London Season wanted to hear about herself.

The irony in her voice went straight over the head of Sir Walter, who in his entire life had never recognized a caustic remark. "And well you should be honored, puss. Marrying into the Warrender family, after all – *the Warrenders.* Quite a step up for the Moores, you know. Your mother would have been in alt – rest her soul. He's willing to be quite generous about the settlements, too."

Some imp of aggravation made her ask, "He is? Lord Henry, you mean?"

"Of course not. I'm talking about Bristol himself. Everybody knows that Harry..." He seemed to think better of what he'd started to say. "Harry... umm..."

"Doesn't have a feather to fly with," Emily finished firmly.

"Well... he *is* a younger son, you know. Of course he doesn't have money of his own. Not that there isn't enough in the family to go around. You needn't ever fret about having a roof over your head, m'girl. Bristol's even talking about making over one of the smaller estates to Harry as a wedding gift."

"How generous of him."

"Well, it is," Sir Walter said, sounding a little defensive. "And I won't deny it's largely because he thinks so highly of you. Told me he was very impressed with you."

Emily didn't bother to ask, this time, which man he was referring to. "Based on what, pray? I've barely met the Marquess of Bristol."

"He said he danced with you once, at some ball or other."

"One country dance, and he decided I'm the right wife for his son? It was Estelle Wilmington's coming-out ball. But I wouldn't expect the Marquess of Bristol to remember that."

"Well, of course not. Busy man and all that. Peer of the realm."

"I suppose I should be flattered that he's put his mind to looking after my future, along with his son's."

"That's right. And no one's ever said Bristol doesn't look after his obligations."

Which is more than his son is likely to do, Emily thought.

"And there will be a nice amount settled on you, personally, as well. For your children, one day."

"Children?" Emily didn't know whether to laugh or cry. "Father, you can't really be serious about marrying me off to Harry Warrender, of all people!"

That was when she knew she'd gone a bit too far – for Sir Walter drew himself up straight and said, "What's that you say, Miss? Begging your pardon, but I've laid out the blunt for three London seasons now, and there's not been an offer worth thinking about despite that dowry your grandmother left you. A fine job *you've* been doing in the marriage sweepstakes!"

Sir Walter, it seemed, understood irony after all.

*****

If it had been only her father who wanted to marry her off, Emily thought she could have talked him around, made him see how utterly ridiculous a notion it was, and shown him the advantages of having an adult daughter still at home to tend to the household and look after his creature comforts.

But there was her stepmother – and Adele, Lady Moore, thought the marriage was a splendid idea.

Sir Walter's second wife was only a few years older than Emily herself, and when he had met Adele on a holiday at Tunbridge Wells, swept her off her feet and to the altar, and brought her home as a bride to Ashton Hall, Emily had thought perhaps they would be friends. After a few days, she'd hoped they could rub along under the same roof without quarreling. After a few weeks, she found herself praying that they could avoid being in the same room. And in a few months, by the time they all went up to London for the season, Emily had never been so glad to see her friends, or to have the distraction of the shops and the lending library and the parties.

Still, Adele seemed to be enjoying herself just as much in London as Emily was. They'd actually started to get along. Adele had even encouraged her to refurbish her wardrobe and to invite her friends to the Moores' town house.

Emily had been blindsided – and wounded – when she realized that Adele was so anxious to get her husband's daughter out of the house that she would push for even such a match as Harry Warrender.

Of course, Emily owned, she wasn't quite being fair to Adele. The second son of a Marquess *was* a good match for the only daughter of a mere baronet, especially one who was several years out of the schoolroom. Even if the groom was a rake who had a long string of actresses, singers, and – if the gossip was correct – bits of fluff to his credit. Even if every young woman who'd made her come-out for the last five years could tell a story, if she chose, of slipping away to a dark corner with Harry Warrender.

Every young woman, it seemed to Emily, except *her*. Harry had never once suggested that they tryst behind a set of velvet portieres, or meet in a dim nook off a ballroom. And he'd never once danced her through a set of french doors onto a forbidden terrace, either.

For what it was worth – which wasn't much – she'd actually been a lot closer to being caught in a compromising position with Harry's father than she ever had been with Harry himself. After that one dance at Estelle Wilmington's coming-out ball, it had seemed for a moment as the music ended that the Marquess of Bristol was going to ask Emily to dance the next with him as well. Two dances in a row – and the second one a waltz ... Yes, that would have had eyebrows raising all over the ballroom. Even at his age, and with his exalted rank, the Marquess couldn't wink at society's rules to that degree.

But of course he hadn't. He wouldn't. Because the busy man, the peer of the realm, had found out all he wanted to know about Emily Moore in one brief dance. She was *sensible*. She was *steady*. What else could he possibly need to know?

*****

She held out for a full week, refusing to discuss the marriage proposal even with her father. Adele, of course, talked of almost nothing else, though to her credit she did no more than drop broad hints to her friends about a wonderful future for Emily. Emily was certain her stepmother's restraint about spreading the news was more in fear of the ultimate embarrassment if the match fell through, rather than any sympathy for Emily's feelings.

But as much as Emily would have liked to return to her old life after the London season, she wasn't a fool. And she had to admit that sharing a house – even her beloved Ashton Hall – with her love-blind father and her simpering stepmother was enough to make nearly any marriage offer look appealing.

Just a week after the Marquess of Bristol's offer, Adele announced that she was increasing, with every hope of finally giving Sir Walter the son he had always wanted. That afternoon, Emily went to her father and agreed to the match. That evening Sir Walter caught up with the Marquess of Bristol at their mutual club. The next day the Marquess sent the betrothal announcement to the newspapers. Only then, for the very first time, did Harry come to call on Emily.

That had been less than a month ago. And the wedding would be on Saturday.

*****

"I wasn't asking about the *day*," Annabelle said, and suddenly Emily's thoughts returned to the ballroom once more. "I know the wedding's on Saturday. I meant, what time?"

"Ten in the morning," Emily said. Her gaze drifted once more to Harry, who was now waltzing with Estelle Wilmington. "It will be a very intimate ceremony, actually, followed by a wedding breakfast. I gather the private chapel is – well, private. Very small."

"Is that why almost nobody's invited? It's all so romantic. Just you and Harry – and then you'll have the rest of your *lives*." Annabelle fussed with the small bunch of violets she carried, straightening the ribbons, sniffing the petals.

Yes, thought Emily drearily. *The rest of our lives...*

"I thought maybe the Marquess didn't want lots of females around, fainting because Harry's not going to be free anymore. All the girls are heartbroken as it is, because after Saturday..." Annabelle took her nose out of her flowers. "Like Estelle, for instance. If I didn't know better, I'd say she's been crying. But she *wouldn't*. Not at a ball."

Emily blinked and looked again. The waltz had ended, but at the edge of the dance floor Harry and Estelle were still in position, his hand lightly resting on the small of her back, her hand clasped in his, as if waiting for the music to start up again so they could keep waltzing.

Their conduct was starting to draw attention. And Annabelle was right, Emily noted. Even from this distance, she could see that Estelle's smile was shaky and her eyes were shadowed.

Emily watched them for a long moment. Then she sighed. *Enough is enough,* she thought. "Excuse me, Annabelle."

"Ooh," Annabelle whispered. "What are you going to *do*, Emily? Oh, pray, you aren't going to make a scene. Are you?"

"No matter how much it may disappoint you when I don't," Emily said crisply, "I have no intention of doing anything of the sort. But come along if you like, and see for yourself."

Annabelle stayed by her side as Emily worked her way slowly across the crowded ballroom, smiling and nodding to acquaintances, on her way toward her wayward betrothed and the hapless young woman who was still standing in the circle of his arms, looking up at him as if he was the moon and all the stars.

When she reached Harry and Estelle, Emily spoke cheer-fully, without lowering her voice. "There you are, Harry. How lovely of you to keep Estelle company while she waited for Annabelle to join her." She linked her arm in Harry's. "It's our dance, I believe, but I am so warm. Let's find a private spot to sit instead – so we can talk."

She kept smiling even as she noted, almost grimly, that he gulped hard before he escorted her toward the ballroom doors, for her first-ever visit to a private nook with Harry.

*****

They were gone from the ballroom for twenty minutes. It was quite long enough for everyone to hear that they had gone out together without a chaperone, and more than enough time for the stories to spread about how Emily had snatched her betrothed from the very arms of another woman. By the time they returned, every eye in the room was watching, and the whispers had become a dull roar.

The girls stared shamelessly, and with envy, at Emily's satisfied smile and the way her hand lay possessively tucked in the bend of Harry's arm. The matrons discreetly checked Emily's dress and hair for signs of damage. The young men darted furtive glances at Harry.

Everyone saw the elegant lift of Emily's hand as she offered it to for Harry to kiss before she turned to her partner for the next dance. Everyone saw Harry standing at the edge of the floor, still looking severely abashed, as she floated off in the arms of a young viscount. And everyone saw that for the rest of the evening, he went nowhere near Estelle Wilmington.

A young buck across the ballroom muttered, "That must have been quite a dressing-down. Poor Harry looks like he's been ten rounds with Gentleman Jackson, but *she's* fresh as a daisy." He shook his head. "Makes a man think twice about parson's mousetrap, egad!"

The Marquess of Bristol, standing in the door of the card room with his elderly cousin Lady Stone, said, "I told you the chit was exactly what he needed. Steady and sensible, that's the ticket. She'll settle him down."

Lady Stone snorted.

*****

It wasn't until her wedding day that Emily saw the Marquess of Bristol's private chapel for the first time, and realized that it was even smaller than she'd been told. There were no pews, but four chairs had been placed at the ready for the Marquess; his eldest son, Lord Southley; Lady Stone; and Adele, Lady Moore. In front of the altar, the bishop – a friend of the Warrender family – waited to perform the ceremony, with the hem of his embroidered robes brushing Lord Southley's well-blacked boots. In the back stood Emily with her father, waiting to make their six-step walk up the aisle.

As the clock in the hallway outside struck ten, the only person missing was the groom.

*****

By eleven, Sir Walter's face was puce; the Marquess's mouth was a rigid line; Lord Southley was lounging low in his chair, quite possibly asleep; Lady Stone was looking thoughtful; Adele was tapping her fingernails on the communion rail; Emily was pale but composed; and the bishop had sat down on a small stool in a corner, carefully arranging his vestments to avoid wrinkles.

Harry was still missing.

Finally Emily spoke, breaking a long and painful silence. "It seems a bit silly to wait any longer."

"I'll banish him to the farthest corner of the globe," the Marquess said under his breath.

"Only if I don't find him first," Sir Walter announced. "Getting my girl's hopes up... making all sorts of promises... leading her on..." He paused, then added gruffly, "Though when it comes right down to it, Bristol, it wasn't Harry who did all that. It was you."

"If you're challenging me to a duel for your daughter's honor, Sir Walter–"

"Nonsense." Emily moved for the first time in an hour. "Obviously, Harry doesn't want to be married. So that's the end of it. "

Lady Stone said, "You seem to be taking it very calmly, girl."

"What other option have I, ma'am?" *Careful, Emily.*

"Steady and sensible," Lady Stone mused. "Isn't that what you called her, Bristol?"

"But now she's *ruined*," Adele wailed. "No decent man will have her! I ought to have suspected. When my friends told me what you did at the Spragues' ball... How you embarrassed Harry... What did you say to him, Emily? I just *know* this is all your fault!"

"Here, now," Sir Walter said. "Adele, m'dear – calm yourself. Not good for the heir, you know."

"Oh, *bother* the heir, Walter. Don't you understand? This chit will be underfoot for all her *life*!"

"I most certainly will not," Emily snapped.

"She'll *never* be married!" Adele lunged out of her chair, fingers clawing at Emily's bouquet.

Suddenly, without seeming to move, the Marquess was between Emily and her stepmother, firmly but gently settling Adele back into her seat. "I think a private conference is called for, to decide what to do next. Sir Walter and I have much to discuss."

Emily opened her mouth, hesitated, and closed it again.

The Marquess's gaze rested thoughtfully on her. "And Miss Moore, of course."

"Jolly idea." Lord Southley yawned and sat up. "Meanwhile, the rest of us will go and start the wedding breakfast."

*****

Sir Walter's book room would have fit in a corner of the Marquess of Bristol's library. Under other circumstances, Emily would have enjoyed browsing the shelves, but she stood stiffly on the carpet in the very center of the room, still clutching her bouquet, until the Marquess took the wilting flowers from her hand and gave her a glass of wine instead. "Sit down. This may take a while to sort out."

Emily eyed him warily, but she remained standing and only sipped the wine.

The Marquess moved easily across the room to fill a glass for her father.

Sir Walter sat down with a groan. "Plaguey rheumatism. What's to be done, Bristol?" he blustered. "That young puppy of yours has ruined my girl!"

"Father..."

"I'm not at all sure of that, Sir Walter," the Marquess said thoughtfully.

"What the blazes do you mean? Of course he's ruined her. Her mother's right."

"Stepmother." Emily couldn't stop herself.

Sir Walter was too far into his rant to notice the interruption. "With Harry's reputation, no decent man will believe she's untouched. And after her performance at the Spragues' ball last week – Oh, yes, my girl; I heard all about it too. I didn't speak up because you were to be married within days. But now–"

"I was there," the Marquess said absently. "At the ball."

"You're surely not saying you were playing gooseberry for them the whole time!"

"No, I wasn't chaperoning. The alcove under the stairs, was it, Miss Moore?"

Emily felt color rise in her cheeks. "Yes, my lord."

He nodded. "I thought as much. It's been a popular little corner of that house since I was Harry's age. I very much doubt that you need worry about Miss Moore being debauched at the Spragues' ball, Sir Walter. It's not *that* private a spot. Unless...." He frowned. "Miss Moore, I must insist on an honest answer. Has my son acted toward you in a way unbecoming a gentleman?"

"No, my lord."

"I'm not just asking about the Spragues' ball, you understand."

Harry was a rake, all right – but not to her. She couldn't throw him to the wolves just because she seemed to have got herself into a spot of trouble. So Emily told the truth. "No, my lord."

"Never?"

She swallowed hard.

"I think I begin to see the light." The Marquess strolled across the room and picked up the wine decanter.

"Well, I'm damned if I do," said Sir Walter. "But as long as you're pouring, my lord, I could use another."

The Marquess topped off Emily's glass as well. "I don't need..." she began.

"No, probably not," he said dryly. "I've seldom seen anyone in less need of Dutch courage than you. Tell me, Miss Moore. What are your plans?"

"Plans?" she asked uneasily.

"She was just jilted, Bristol. I hardly think the girl has *plans*!"

"Her stepmother does not believe she was jilted," the Marquess said thoughtfully.

"Well," Sir Ralph began. "Adele gets these notions..."

"And *I* do not believe she was jilted," the Marquess went on.

Sir Walter sputtered and choked, and climbed awkwardly to his feet once more. "What the blazes? Bristol–"

"Drink your wine, my dear girl," said the Marquess, "and tell me what you and Harry were talking about at the ball. What caused you to look so very pleased with yourself, and made it seem he'd been bitten by his favorite dog?"

"Estelle Wilmington," she said with relief. *Back on firm ground at last*, she thought. "Harry had been paying her far too much attention, and I ended it."

His eyebrow lifted. "Ended the attention? Or ended the betrothal?"

Before Emily could stop herself, she'd winced. Damn the man, did he have to be quite so acute?

"Ah," he said. "I see."

Emily found herself feeling a reluctant admiration. He obviously *did* see – a great deal too much for her taste – while her father was still looking befuddled. She gave up and drained her wineglass. "All right then. I asked Harry if he was as serious about Estelle as she obviously was about him."

"She'd been crying that night," the Marquess said thoughtfully.

Emily shot him a look. He'd seen *that*? "And he said that he rather thought he loved her, but you'd told him if he didn't marry me, you'd cut off his allowance, and disown him, and I don't know what all."

"Horsewhips may have been mentioned," the Marquess said mildly.

"So I suggested that he just disappear for a while and I'd break the news to you."

"In the fond belief that it would make me less angry to hear it from you?"

But he didn't sound angry, Emily thought. He sounded ... No, surely he couldn't be amused.

"And why did you wait several more days, until you were actually standing in front of the altar, to inform me? Once again, Miss Moore, I ask: *What are your plans?* I do not believe that you didn't consider what you would do afterwards, when you and Harry set up your little scheme to dodge a wedding. No, let me rephrase that. When *you* set up your little scheme. I very much doubt Harry had much to say about it. Did you expect a nice settlement from me, to soothe your broken heart?"

He was *not* amused, then. She'd been quite wrong about that.

Her face was aflame, her throat raw. "No! I certainly did not." She swallowed hard. "My grandmother left me a small inheritance. It's enough to support me, if I live very quietly."

"I would never agree to that," Sir Walter blustered. "And neither would your mother."

"Stepmother," Emily said again. "And I know quite well that neither you nor she would approve of me setting up my own establishment. But Adele hasn't been trying to marry me off just to get me out of her house. She also wants to use me to form some kind of grand alliance." She took a deep breath. "So I thought if there was enough of a scandal that no man would be interested in me, then no one would mind very much if I went off to live on my own."

Sir Walter sat down rather suddenly. "So you've ruined yourself."

"I'm truly sorry for hurting you, Father. But it seemed to me there was no other way." Emily put down the empty glass she'd been clutching.

"I'll make it right, Sir Walter. But it's not only your reputation which has been injured, Miss Moore. My family's honor is at stake. "

"My lord," she said warily, "I do most sincerely regret... It was not my intention to injure your name."

"Any more than Harry already has, you mean." He smiled a little. "You were promised marriage into the Warrender family, Miss Moore. And that is what you shall have. There are other Warrenders. My son Southley..."

"Oh, no!" Despite her best efforts, Emily couldn't choke back her wail.

"You would be a marchioness one day."

"But that would be disgusting, sitting around waiting for you to die so that someday..." Her voice gave out. "No. It is most kind of you to be concerned about my future, but there's no need. And in any case, Southley would have something to say about that."

"Just as Harry did?"

Was it her imagination, or was there a twinkle in his dark eyes?

"Well, perhaps you're right about Southley," the Marquess mused. "Since he seems more interested in the wedding breakfast than in the wedding, that may be answer enough. So that leaves just one choice, really."

"Eh?" Sir Walter asked.

"Being a marchioness now, rather than later."

Emily's heart was skipping madly in her chest.

"Will you marry me, Miss Moore?"

Sir Walter said, "*What?*"

Her throat was so tight she could barely speak. "I think your sense of honor has run away with you, my lord. That's quite–" She stopped suddenly.

The Marquess said, "Sir Walter, under the circumstances, may I have a few minutes alone with your daughter?"

In desperation, Emily reverted to childhood habits. "Papa!"

But Sir Walter seemed not to hear her. "Certainly, my lord." He departed, with alacrity.

The silence in the library seemed to smother her. In the fireplace, a log cracked and fell, and Emily jumped as if a shotgun had gone off.

"You were saying?" the Marquess prompted. "My offer is ... Unnecessary? Insulting? Ridiculous? Medieval?– Pray tell me what you were going to say, before good manners made you pause."

She said quietly, "Because your son didn't wish to marry me does not mean that you must make yourself a sacrifice, my lord."

He smiled a little. "Certainly not."

"Then it's settled." She looked around. "Perhaps... Might I have another glass of wine, before..."

"Before you have to face your stepmother? I think not. I'd rather receive your answer when you're not foxed."

"But I've answered. You can't ask me to marry you based on one dance, months ago."

He looked thoughtful, and too late, Emily realized what she had said. She shouldn't even have *remembered* that one dance, much less let him guess that it might have been special.

"A few minutes ago," the Marquess said, "you expressed surprise that I had noticed Miss Wilmington crying, at the Spragues' ball."

She was equally startled that he'd noticed her reaction. "What about it?"

"I noticed because it affected you – as I've noticed everything which has affected you in the last few months. In fact, it was my intention to take Harry to task for the way he had treated you at the Spragues' ball. But… I didn't."

"Because everyone thought I already had." There was a trace of bitterness in Emily's voice.

"No. Because – I've only now realized – I didn't want things to go well between you and Harry. That despite everything I'd done, everything I'd arranged, I wanted you for myself." He paused. "When you said, a few minutes ago, that it would be disgusting to you to wait for me to die – there was something in your tone…"

She bit her lip.

He let the silence draw out, and when finally he spoke again, his voice became a little heavier. "But of course I understand your reaction. The age difference. If my offer is repulsive to you, we'll work out something else to save your reputation, Miss Moore."

She should thank him prettily, and curtsey, and go back out to face her stepmother. But Emily didn't move. She told herself it was because she'd promised Harry to argue his case with his father. But instead she said, "It's not, exactly. Repulsive, I mean. And it's not a matter of age. There must be a bigger difference between my father and Adele."

"True," he said meditatively. "And just look how well that's going."

She bubbled over with laughter – and hope – and a sudden frisson of possibility. "Well, yes. I think part of her fondness for Harry was the fact that he's only a second son, so I wouldn't outrank her."

"And you really don't mind that Harry seems to prefer Estelle?"

Emily shook her head. "He's a dear boy, really. An engaging scamp, when he puts his mind to it."

The Marquess smiled. "I do hope you didn't tell him that, at the Spragues' ball."

"He just needs the right woman," she said firmly.

"As do I, my dear. So Lady Moore will be livid at the idea that you're to be a marchioness?"

"*Am* I going to be?" Emily's voice quivered a little. "Are you absolutely certain that you're not just feeling a sense of duty?"

"Yes, my dear – I am certain. If you can bear me, that is. I've come to my senses. It wasn't Harry I wanted you for, it was always me."

"And I..." She paused, and then said very softly, "I almost hated you for that dance, you know. It was so lovely – so very right. And then... never again."

"If I hadn't walked away from you that very moment, I never would have. I wanted to stay with you. But a girl your age, and an old man like me..."

"Not so very old," she whispered. And then, after he kissed her, "Not old at all."

He laughed and held her closer. "A special license, I think. I'm in no mood to wait. If that's all right?"

"Oh, yes. Very much all right." Emily tucked her hand into his arm and said, "I might even forgive Harry now, for what he told me at the Spragues' ball."

"Exactly what did my graceless son say?"

"He said talking to me was like being scolded by his mother."

The Marquess of Bristol laughed. "Harry has no taste. Remind me, the next time we have occasion to visit the Spragues, to show you the real value of that alcove under the stairs."

"Couldn't you just show me here in the library?" Emily asked wistfully.

And it was a great deal later when he and his future marchioness rejoined their guests.

The Tattooed Lady

Beth settled her sunshade in place and retied her shoes, waiting for Ginny to finish her stretches. "Come on, girlfriend. Let's get going."

Ginny stood on one foot and bent her other knee till her heel nearly touched her thigh. "You weren't so impatient to get out on the path and start sweating last week. What's going on?"

"Nothing. I just want to get our walk in early so I can have dinner ready by the time Josh gets off duty."

Ginny straightened her knee, retied her trendy scarf at the throat of her pink warm-up suit, and started off down the walking path. "Everything all right between you and Josh?"

Of course Ginny would go right to the heart of things. She had an uncanny gift for that. Beth shrugged, trying to make the gesture look careless. "What could go wrong?"

"Well, it wouldn't be unheard of for the honeymoon to be over. Three months of marriage does that to a lot of couples."

"Not us," Beth said. She picked up the pace a little and told herself that the tightness in her breathing was just because she hadn't been patient enough today to warm up her muscles before starting to walk. It had nothing to do with the extra five pounds she'd acquired since her Christmas wedding. And it also had nothing to do with the fact that Josh had volunteered to swap a shift and fill in for another firefighter today, even though this was their three-month anniversary.

"You'll forgive me if I mention that your voice sounds a little hollow when you say that." Ginny waved at an acquaintance a hundred yards away, on the next loop of the walking path. "It's none of my business, of course. And I'm not trying to get rid of you,

Beth, but maybe you should start taking walks with Josh sometimes instead of with me."

"He'd rather go for a run. He says it's efficient – he gets more exercise in a shorter time frame."

"You mean he thinks walks are boring?"

No, Beth thought almost bitterly. *I'm afraid he thinks I'm boring.*

Ginny was watching her with narrowed eyes. "I hear they've hired a new firefighter at the station. A new *female* firefighter."

"She scored highest of all the new applicants, Josh said. And she passed all the tests."

Ginny raised an eyebrow. "But before they can get hired, don't they have to – like – pick up another firefighter and carry him out of a building?"

"Yeah."

"And she did that? Wow. What does this woman look like, King Kong?"

"I haven't seen her yet," Beth admitted.

"What's stopping you? I make it a point to check out every new teller at the bank, just so I know exactly who Joe has hired lately and whether any of them are likely to put the moves on him to spend lunch hours in the vault."

"That's a sexist attitude."

"It sure is," Ginny said comfortably. "And if Joe hired tellers on the basis of their attractiveness, it would be worse than sexist, it'd be illegal. But I'm not the one who hires them – and there's nothing wrong with a woman keeping an eye on her husband."

"It's easy for you. You have a good excuse for going into the bank every few days."

"Like you can't come up with a reason to stop by the fire station to see your husband? What kind of a wuss are you, girl? Take over some snacks for the guys. They love your chocolate-chip cookies."

"Everybody loves my chocolate-chip cookies." *Including me, which is one of the reasons I'm out here sweating this afternoon.* How many miles would she have to walk to get rid of that extra five pounds, anyway? And would it make any difference?

That's thinking like a loser, Beth told herself. *And I'm not a loser.*

Not yet, anyway.

*****

Their three-month anniversary dinner was ready by the time Josh's shift was over. A creamy asparagus soup – almost like the one they'd shared on the last night of their honeymoon – was simmering on the stove, the yeast rolls were in the oven, and the prime-cut steaks were ready for the barbecue grill. Beth glanced at the clock and went to tidy her hair and freshen her makeup. It took only ten minutes to drive from the central fire station to their house, and she wanted to look her very best when Josh arrived.

Ten minutes went by. Fifteen. A half hour.

An hour.

The soup curdled. Beth was pouring the last of it down the drain when Josh finally came in. She barely heard the back door bang because of the roar of the garbage disposal.

"Sorry I'm late," he said.

"What kept you?" Beth's voice was steady; she was proud of herself.

"Farrah wanted to review procedure for a toxic spill. We do things a bit differently than she learned at the training center. Good, you haven't started making dinner. I want a shower first." He aimed a kiss at her ear, missed, and went off down the hall, whistling.

You haven't started making dinner? She stood there with the pan in her hand and thought about hitting him with it. The roar of the blood in her ears almost drowned out the garbage disposal.

She put the steaks on the grill, pulled the rolls out of the oven, and waited.

In less than ten minutes he was back, wearing fresh jeans and a Lakewood fire department tee shirt, with his hair still dark with water and curling gently against his neck. He put his arms around her and kissed her deeply.

Beth's heart melted. He was so very handsome – so alive, so much fun, so sexy. And he was hers. Sometimes she had to peek at his left hand – at the gold wedding ring he always wore when he was off duty – just to make herself believe that of all the women in Lakewood, Josh had chosen her.

She was no beauty, and Beth knew it. She was shorter than average, so every extra ounce seemed to show. Her hair was plain brown, her eyes were ordinary blue. And she was a teacher at the local preschool, with just one class of four-year-olds each morning – so her after-work conversation was seldom very exciting, either.

As if he'd read her mind, Josh asked, "How was school today?"

"Jamie head-butted Ryan in the tummy in a squabble over their favorite swing, and Ryan threw up."

"So just another normal day at preschool then, huh?" He lifted the corner of the dishtowel which covered the yeast rolls and took a deep breath. "Man, that smells good. And steaks? What's the occasion?"

"Nothing special," she teased. "I was just thinking about where we were three mon..." She stopped suddenly, mid-word.

"Where we were... when?"

"No big deal," Beth said. And she told herself it *wasn't* a big deal. He'd just forgotten, that was all. He'd been in a hurry after his shower because he was rushing to get back to her.

That must be why – for the first time she could recall – he hadn't put on his wedding ring.

*****

Josh didn't wear his heavy gold band at work, of course. A ring on a man's hand could be dangerous, he had explained. Too many firefighters had lost fingers when their rings caught on equipment, or on the unpredictable loose edges that were always a hazard at a fire scene. Because of one particularly horrible accident many years ago, the Lakewood fire department had decreed that firefighters were not allowed to wear jewelry on the job.

Beth, who loved Josh's big, strong hands, had shuddered at the idea of one of his long, expressive fingers being torn away. So though she had bought him a wedding ring and had it engraved with their names and wedding date, she made sure the box it had come in was always right on top of his dresser – so he could easily put the ring away when he got ready for work and easily find it when he came home again.

And he always had. Until tonight.

She told herself she was being ridiculous. But the next day, as soon as she was home from her morning preschool class, she mixed up a batch of chocolate-chip batter. When the first two pans to come out of the oven had cooled enough to handle, she slid the cookies onto a big glass platter and drove to the fire station.

The overhead doors were open to the early spring sunshine, and as always, the two big fire trucks stood ready with doors open and turnout gear in place.

"I brought treats," she called as she went in, blinking a bit as she walked from sunshine into shadow.

A couple of firemen were polishing the brass rails on the oldest of the fire engines, which was now more of a relic than a useful piece of equipment. Fred – the more experienced of the two – nudged the other fireman and said, "Go get the captain, Hank."

Was there something a little guilty about Fred's tone? Surely not. Beth's imagination had gone into overdrive, that was all.

"I'll get him," Beth said brightly. "Is he in the kitchen?"

"No. He's back in the gym," Hank admitted.

She set the plate of cookies down on the step of the fire engine and walked across the garage to a small storage area. Last fall, the guys had spent their own time and money cleaning the room out, painting the walls, and fitting it up as a workout space. But now that the weather was nicer, why was Josh spending time in a cramped, makeshift, airless gym when he could be outdoors?

He can't exactly run five miles when he's on duty, Beth reminded herself. A firefighter had to be right beside the truck when an alarm came in, or he wasn't much use.

Josh was in the gym, all right, but he wasn't alone. He was standing at the head of a padded bench, spotting for the weightlifter on the bench. The moment Beth saw who was lying there, gripping the heavy iron bar, her internal sirens went off, louder than any fire alarm she'd ever heard.

"Hey," Josh said. "What brings you down here in the middle of the day?"

He didn't sound guilty, she noted. He also didn't sound terribly interested in Beth as he helped the woman on the bench guide the bar back into the rests.

"Chocolate-chip cookies," Beth said. She couldn't take her eyes off the woman as she sprang up from the bench as gracefully as if she was dismounting from a balance beam.

On her right shoulder blade, clearly visible beside the strap of the skimpiest black tank top Beth had ever seen, was a tattoo. Before Beth could spot what it was, the woman slung a towel over her shoulder and turned around.

She was tall – at least six inches taller than Beth. She had white-blonde hair, cut very short in an upswept, angular style that suited her elfin face and high cheekbones. She had huge blue-violet eyes and a build that could have graced the red carpet at the Oscars. There was certainly no doubt about her being female, and she obviously didn't need padding in the flesh-colored sports bra which peeked though the armhole of the tank top.

Josh said, "Beth, this is Farrah, our newest team member. Farrah, this is Beth."

Not *This is my wife*. She was just – *Beth*, she noted woodenly.

Farrah advanced, holding out her hand. "So nice to meet you." Then she seemed to think better of it and wiped her palm vigorously on the towel. "Sorry – I'm pretty hot and sweaty."

Far more *pretty* than *hot and sweaty*, Beth thought.
"How do you like the fire department so far?"

"Oh, it's great. The guys have been wonderful. Very welcoming."

"Did you say you brought cookies?" Josh asked. "I hope you didn't leave them with Hank, or they'll all be gone." He led the way out of the workout room.

Beth didn't object; the room had seemed to be too small for the three of them.

"Hey, guys, leave some of those for the rest of us," Josh called across the garage to Hank and Fred.

"We were just sampling while they were still warm," Hank said. "Captain, I've got an idea. We need to raise funds for some more equipment for the gym. Maybe we could have a bake sale."

"Just don't look at me," Farrah said pleasantly. "I don't bake. I'll pull my share of kitchen duty the same way all you guys do, but be warned – you'd rather have me washing dishes than cooking."

Beth was torn between respect and irritation. Farrah had made it clear in a heartbeat that she wasn't going to be the fire station's maid or cook just because she was the only female – and putting that bunch of guys in their place with a smile was a feat to be celebrated. On the other hand, baking a few cookies wouldn't kill her, would it? What was so wrong with the traditional female pursuits?

Josh held out the plate. Farrah hesitated, then took a cookie. The toned, well-defined muscles in her arm flexed under tanned skin as she broke it in two and took a tiny bite. She stood like a sculpted ballerina, Beth thought, with one toe pointed out.

The cookie platter made another round.

"Hey, guys, leave a cookie for Farrah," Josh warned.

"If she's going to be just one of the guys," Hank said, "let her fight for her own."

Farrah shook her head. "They're really good, Beth. But if I ate another one, I'd have to go straight back to the gym." She laughed. "Or pick Josh up again and carry him up a flight or two of steps."

Again? It was *Josh* she'd carried during that training test? Beth felt chilly. She looked down at the cookie in her hand. She didn't remember taking it off the platter, much less crunching it into a ball in her fist.

"I'm going to go hit the treadmill for a few minutes," Farrah said.

In silence, they all watched her walk away. Definitely the woman was a dancer, Beth thought. She let her gaze drift from one man to the next, avoiding looking at Josh.

Hank must have noticed her watching him as he watched Farrah. He turned slightly red and said hastily, "What kind of a flower is that on her back, anyway?"

"It's a tulip," Beth said.

"Odd sort of tattoo for a firefighter to have," Fred said. "I thought about getting one once. Crossed hose nozzles. Maybe I will someday."

Hank reached out a long arm and took another cookie. "If I was to get a tattoo, I'd make it a chocolate chip."

"That would just end up looking like a cowpie," Josh said. "Heck, maybe we should make it a team thing and everybody go get one."

Beth saw red. "Get a *tattoo*? You have *never* said a word about wanting a–"

The fire alarm shrilled.

Hank shoved the rest of his cookie in his mouth, stepped into his turnout gear, and while still pulling on his coat, climbed behind the wheel of the nearest fire truck. Fred seized his gear and headed for the other truck. Josh picked up the phone to get the dispatcher's instructions. Farrah seemed to soar across the garage, into her gear, and up into the truck's back seat.

Beth waited till the engines had cleared the station before she walked back to her car. She didn't realize until after the doors had automatically closed that Josh had picked up the cookie platter off the step of the fire truck and handed it to her.

She ate the rest of the cookies as she drove home.

*****

"A tulip," Beth told Ginny that afternoon. "She has a pink tulip, tattooed on her shoulder blade. Talk about obvious. A *tulip*!"

"Well, at least she doesn't have a pair of them. You know, *two lips*."

"For all I know, she does. Though I don't think there was enough of her covered up to hide a whole flower. A petal would probably have peeked out somewhere – unless the thing's on her derriere. No, I'd have seen it if it was, because her pants were so tight the outline of the ink would have shown!"

Ginny was panting. "Slow down, Beth. Your aggravation is making you walk so fast I can't keep up."

"And now Josh is talking about getting a tattoo. My Josh – wanting a tattoo!"

"He must have just been acting polite. You know – making conversation. She's the new kid on the block, so he wants her to feel comfortable. It's part of his job, as the supervisor. It doesn't mean he *meant* it."

Beth shook her head. "I don't buy that. If it was Joe welcoming one of his new bank tellers by suggesting that everyone go get stabbed with inky needles, would you say he was just making polite conversation?"

"I can't imagine Joe and inky needles in the same sentence," Ginny admitted, "much less the same room."

"Anyway, I'm going to talk to Josh tonight. If she's going to be just one of the boys, then she's going to have to behave like one of the boys. She can't have it both ways."

"Good luck," Ginny said softly. "But sweetie – be careful. Don't go saying things you haven't thought all the way through."

"The honeymoon's over, Ginny."

"Yeah. That's exactly what I mean."

*****

Josh's SUV was already in the garage when Beth got home from the park, and he was in the kitchen with a glass of wine standing on the counter beside him.

"Hey," he said as she came in. He stopped unpacking a grocery bag and casually draped an arm around her shoulders.

Beth fended him off. "I'm all sweaty from my walk."

"I don't care. But I'll wait if you want a shower first, or a long bubble bath." He put the wine glass in her hand.

"Were we out of pretzels and ice cream? Since when do you do the grocery shopping, anyway?"

"It's a special occasion. Our ninety-day anniversary."

Beth's heart fluttered. "*You remembered*?"

"I'm making you that pasta carton thing you liked on our honeymoon."

"It was pasta carbonara. Do you even know what ingre-dients go into pasta carbonara?"

"I may have come close," Josh admitted.

"Anyway, it's *not* our anniversary – that was yesterday. I know what happened, Josh," she said sadly. "You finally realized why I was cooking steaks last night, so you decided to pretend it was today instead to get yourself off the hook."

"It *is* today," he insisted. "The end of December to the end of March, plus two days because February only has twenty-eight, means it's ninety days ago today that we got married. That's why I swapped shifts and worked yesterday, so I could be off early today. You'll never guess what I got you."

Beth's head was swimming. She wasn't about to dig out a calendar and count; the fact that Josh had made the calculations made her feel warm all over. Three months; ninety days... who cared which of them was actually right? Maybe they both were. He *had* remembered, after all.

"Is it gold?" she asked.

"Nope."

"Platinum?"

"Nope. Much more meaningful than that."

"Nothing's more meaningful than platinum," she teased. Not that she cared; she was savoring the glow. She felt like her whole insides had lit up. How she loved this man! "Don't tell me you went traditional and got me something paper, because that's for the first year, not the first three months."

"I got you a tattoo," he said.

Beth's glow died into ashes. "You did *what*? You want me to let someone stick inky needles into me? I suppose you've already picked out the artwork I should wear for the rest of my life, too. Well, I have something to say about that, Josh. How about the outline of a hand with the middle finger extended?"

"No, dear. No needles for you."

"Then what are you talking about?"

He held up a hand. His left hand. And again, he wasn't wearing his wedding ring.

She looked closer. "You hurt your hand," she said uncertainly.

"You can say that again – wicked painful it was. I'm supposed to keep it covered till it heals, but I wanted you to see it. Look closer."

The skin at the base of his ring finger looked angry – red and swollen. But inside the puffy area was a darker shadow, a wide gold-colored streak which went all the way around.

"It's a wedding ring I never have to take off," Josh said. "So there will never be any doubt, no matter where I go, that I'm yours."

Beth didn't know she was crying until he brushed tears away with his thumb.

"Though if you'd *like* to engrave my name inside a big old heart on your tush, Bethie, I could certainly get used to..."

She swatted him. Then she kissed him, hard, and she no longer cared a bit that she was sweaty from her walk.

Blind Date

The last page she read was as dreadful as the first ones had been. The only good thing about her new assignment, Bonnie reflected, was that she didn't have to read entire books, only short stories.

She groaned, and from the neighboring cubicle, Janet said, "Another stinker?"

"From the first line to the last. But I was so much in awe of the author's ability to stack clichés I simply couldn't stop reading. Listen to this. They meet when the heroine bumps her car into the hero's. When she gets out to check the damage, she slams into his chest and drops her purse at his feet. He retrieves her birth control pills and a strip of condoms – and then she bumps her head on his chin when she stands up."

"Does she tumble off a ladder for him to catch?"

"No, but she falls over a fire hydrant, turns her ankle, and has to be carried. When he picks her up, she feels a lightning bolt go through her at his touch …"

"But only the romantic kind of lightning bolt, I assume?"

"Unfortunately, yes; I was wishing for a storm to put her out of her misery. And so on, until seventy-nine clichés later, the heroine sees fireworks as the hero kisses her." Bonnie tossed the story into her out-box for the secretary to deal with. "As if that's the way falling in love works in real life!"

Janet looked sympathetic. "Who does your godmother want you to meet this time?"

Bonnie blinked. "What? Why do you think—"

"Because you only dress up and wear stiletto heels when your godmother's summoned you to lunch at

Spinoli's, and you only sound this cynical when she's arranged a date for you."

Bonnie sighed. "Kevin. He's her dentist."

"Dentist? Hey, if you ever need implants or crowns, it might be handy to be dating a–"

Bonnie caught sight of the clock, grabbed her portfolio, and stuffed it full of stories. Perhaps after lunch she'd find a spot to sit outside and read.

Traffic was heavy, and the street in front of Spinoli's was clogged with taxis. Still half a block from the restaurant, Bonnie dug her wallet out. "Maybe if I get out here, you can swing around the jam." She handed the cabbie the fare and pushed open the door.

He snorted and took his foot off the brake. The strap of Bonnie's portfolio caught on the door handle, and she stumbled as she tried to pull it free. It caught tight, then snapped, and she bounced off the open door and into a man strolling down the sidewalk.

"Oof," he said.

Bonnie's portfolio went spinning across the sidewalk, and she only remained upright because of the hard grip of his hand on her arm.

"Sorry." She bent to pick up the stories, scattered across the concrete as the breeze fluttered the loose pages. She didn't re-alize he'd stooped to help, but when she straightened with her hands full, her elbow struck the top of his head. "Sorry," she said once more.

As she realized what was happening, she started to laugh. A car accident, a dropped bag, a bumped head… this was just like that ridiculous, improbable story she'd been reading, as though it had come to life.

"Excuse me?"

"I'm not laughing at you. I'm an editor, and this is just like one of the stories I was reading. But never mind. Don't let me hold you up."

"No point in getting into line at Spinoli's just now."

Bonnie glanced toward the restaurant, where the line stretched down the sidewalk. There were a dozen young men waiting, and she could think of absolutely no reason to suspect that this one was here to meet her godmother. But there had been so many coincidences already, what was one more?

"Let me guess," she said. "Your name is Kevin. And you're a dentist."

His eyebrows arched. "How'd you know?"

Because I've just walked into the middle of a very badly written romance novel, that's how.

On the other hand, maybe her godmother's taste in men was improving.

She stuffed the pages he handed her into the bulging portfolio and turned toward Spinoli's. Something cracked under her foot and she staggered.

Kevin grabbed her arm again.

"Thanks." Bonnie wiggled her ankle experimentally. The crack she'd heard was the heel of her shoe coming loose.

She rolled her eyes. *Okay, I surrender. I promise never to bad-mouth another story, no matter how many tired plot devices it uses, if I can only get through this lunch.*

At least the heel hadn't broken off entirely, so if she planted her foot carefully with every step, she might still be able to walk.

"Come on," Kevin said. "Lean on me."

"I could just kick my shoes off."

"And take a chance of stepping on broken glass?" He put a hand firmly under her arm, and Bonnie limped toward the entrance.

The maitre d' beamed. "Miss Mason, we have Mrs. Elliot's table ready, but—"

He cast an appraising eye at Kevin, and Bonnie said hastily, "This is Mrs. Elliot's friend Kevin."

Kevin said, "Actually…"

"…Yes, I know, you're her dentist, not exactly her friend. Close enough." She started toward her godmother's favorite table.

It was empty. Well, wasn't that peachy? Setting up a blind date was annoying enough, but for the woman not to appear at all…

The maitre d' went on, "Mrs. Elliot called a few minutes ago. She and her guest have been delayed."

"But he's standing right…" Something clicked in Bonnie's brain, and she tugged her arm free and looked up at the man standing beside her. "Your name isn't really Kevin, is it?"

"Well – no. But you seemed so certain that it would have been a shame to disappoint you."

Bonnie wanted to crawl under the table.

"I suppose I could change it, if you like," he mused. "But – do you insist on me being Kevin? Would something else do?"

"Yes. Anything else. *Please* don't be Kevin. What *is* your name, anyway?"

"Jed Stone."

"Of course. It would have to sound like a hero's."

"You think it does? Really?" He smiled, and Bonnie felt warmth stream through her.

But wasn't that just the way her luck usually ran? – she'd finally met a *good* blind date, only he was the wrong man. "I suppose you're meeting someone."

Jed held her chair and pulled out the one across from her. "I think that I already have." He reached across the table to touch her hand.

As his fingertips gently brushed her skin, Bonnie felt a tingle. Not a lightning bolt exactly, but definitely an electrical sizzle.

Maybe, after all, this *was* how falling in love worked in real life. Because, from the corner of her eye, she caught a glimpse of… fireworks.

A Note from the Author

Thank you for reading this book!

Something I've always enjoyed is tying my books together with little details, threads that run through several stories. Even titles that aren't part of a series will have little Easter eggs here and there – casual connections that I hope will entertain the attentive reader without annoying someone who's picked up just one book.

Things like restaurants, hotels, and stores tend to show up in multiple books, and occasionally a character from a previous book will have a walk-on role in another story. Most of my contemporary heroines wear Midnight Passion perfume and Milady Lingerie; both of those products (as well as many others) first appeared in their own stories and then drifted through other books.

All of my 80 contemporary romance novels are connected in a complex spider web.

So there was no question when I began writing historical romances that I would link all those books together as well.

Of course the main connector in my Regency romances is Lady Stone – that unrepentant old harridan, the most notorious gossip in London – who appears in every one of them. Sometimes she's a major character, sometimes only a walk-on, but she's always somewhere in the mix.

But there are other bits that overlap as well. Minor characters appear in various stories -- the Carew sisters who are a big part of *Her Wedding Wager* first appeared in *The Birthday Scandal*.

At the end of *An Affair for the Season,* James and Julia attend Lady Stone's ball, in her house on Grosvenor Square. Lady Stone's companion, the one who's discovered *in flagrante delicto* in the music room, is Portia Langford from *Just One Season in London.*

The beautiful blonde debutante James admires in the park is Sophie Ryecroft, who also finds her forever love in *Just One Season in London.*

The house just off Portman Square that James tries to borrow for a tryst is the hideaway located at Number Five, Upper Seymour Street, which first appeared in *The Mistress' House.*

But those are just a few of the Easter eggs waiting to be found. I hope you'll have as much fun looking as I did in hiding them!

LEIGH MICHAELS

Leigh Michaels is the award-winning and international best-selling author of more than 100 books, including historical romance, contemporary romance, non-fiction and local history.

More than 35 million copies of her books have been printed in 25 languages and more than 120 countries. Six of her books have been finalists in the Romance Writers of America RITA contest.

She is the author of *Writing the Romance Novel,* now in its fifth edition, which has been called the definitive guide to writing romance novels.

She is a writing teacher, a writing coach, an editor, and a mentor to other writers.

Her interests include collecting and making miniatures for her dollhouse.

For a complete list of her books visit

leighmichaels.com

Sensual and sophisticated
Regency-period historical romance
Their Makeshift Marriage
Gentleman in Waiting
Ruining the Rake
The Birthday Scandal
The Wedding Affair
Just One Season in London
The Mistress' House

Heartwarming and award-winning
contemporary romance
Return to Amberley
The Lake Effect
The Daddy Trap
Traveling Man
Ties that Bind
Family Secrets

Tasty and intriguing
non-fiction
For the Love of Tea
Another Taste of Love
Writing the Romance Novel
Creating Romantic Characters
Writing Between the Sexes
The Dahls' House
Much Ado About Shakespeare

www.ingramcontent.com/pod-product-compliance
Lightning Source LLC
Chambersburg PA
CBHW070927250626
47159CB00009B/3156